Peggy of the Cove
A legend brought to reality

Ivan Fraser

Canadian Cataloguing-in-Publication Data

Fraser, Ivan, 1945-
Peggy of the Cove: a legend brought to reality / Ivan Fraser
ISBN 0-9736872-0-9

Peggy of the Cove (Softcover)
ISBN 0-9736872-2-3

1. Title

PS8611.R38P44 2004   C813'.6   C2004-906321-9

Ivan Fraser (Publisher)
Barbara Webber - Dragon Smoke Ink - Editor

Ivan Fraser Studio
Peggy of the Cove ® Pending
10236 Peggy's Cove Road
Glen Margaret, NS B3Z 3J1
902 823-2083   ivanfraser@peggyscove.net   www.peggyscove.net

Cover Design - Brent Kawolzak - Crossbow International

Printed and bound in Canada by Friesens,
Altona, Manitoba, Canada R0G 0B0

Dedication

Dedicated in memory of Evelyn and Stanley Fraser, Mom and Dad.

When young, seldom do we realize how the qualities inherited from our parents influence the decisions we make, shape our character, or awaken dormant talents as we journey through life. Recently this striking reality hit me.

Mom wrote letters until a few days before her death, December 16, 2003. It always amused me that Florence Hubley and Mom wrote letters often. They lived only a few miles apart. She loved getting mail. Obviously Florence was of the same mind since letters flowed in both directions. Mom kept diaries along with guest books and scrap books galore. If you ever needed to know who married whom, died, or had any interesting stories, she would go through piles of paper to find the answer. Not only was her mind sharp, but she wisely kept good records. We could never go wrong by giving Mom pens, writing paper and stamps for any occasion. She was the Communication Secretary for the Tantallon Seventh-day Adventist Church for years as well as the appointee to send Get well or Sympathy cards to the sick or bereaved.

This God given talent must have rubbed off on me because I still shake my head in disbelief as I see this book and listen to the song I composed, *Peggy of the Cove.* English was not my best subject in school. Thinking about that makes me smile and no doubt Mom would be pleased.

Dad was a very practical man. I'll never forget the night I asked for his car to visit my closest friend, John Merrimen. I needed help with Geometry. Dad wanted to know what my problem was so I showed him the picture of an equilateral triangle. I have to prove that these two angles are equal. His reply was, "Well any fool can see they are." I did get the car.

When Dad was six years old, his father, mother, sister, baby and the maid all died in one week from the flu of 1918. His grandfather and oldest sister, Marjorie raised Dad and his three brothers. By the time he was sixteen, all had left home for work and his grandfather had passed away. Single handed, at that tender age, he remained on the homestead taking care of chickens, cattle, cutting wood and planting gardens. The farmland was kept in immaculate condition as he toiled from daylight to dark.

When he started courting Mom, it wasn't long before he told her it was too cold in winter walking two miles to visit her. Especially climbing that steep hill. After only a few dates, Dad gave Mom a box of chocolates. Grandpop said to her, "you took the bait, now marry him." Shortly after, Dad proposed and they were married. Their courtship makes me chuckle.

Dad had fears the family name wouldn't be carried on, but he did his part with three sons and one daughter. He also was concerned about the family property. His brothers sold or signed over their share to him. There were a few small parcels of land owned by his second cousin, Emmy, who lived next door. He purchased those from her since one jotted into his line and two were in the middle of the fields. Aunt Marjorie kept her fifth until her early nineties when she signed it over to Mom. Every summer she came home from Boston for her vacation. Her room is still like it was then. Matter of fact, that's the room Peggy stayed in when she went to visit Janet in my story.

Never seeing any of his children until they were a week or more old, Dad thought children were like kittens when it came to their eyes being closed at birth. When our daughter Bethanne was born, he came over to see her. She was only a few days old. "Well look at that," he said, "She has her eyes open already."

Dad would be very pleased to know the land has remained in the Fraser family name. You can now visit the home and see the place where in my story, Peggy came to spend time with Janet. It is an art gallery along with the giftware of *Peggy of the Cove*. Visitors are encouraged to walk up Fraser's Hill and enjoy the fabulous view overlooking St. Margaret's Bay.

Mom and Dad on or about their wedding day sitting on the front step of our home. Mom is in her wedding dress. On the back of the photo is written, "Isn't the kitten cute."

Contents

Introduction

Believe it or not, this book is the result of a hurricane.

Josephine was her name. The year was 1996. As an artist, I was intrigued by the effects of this hurricane and naturally took myself down the road to Peggy's Cove. Subsequently, I snapped numerous shots of the waves at the Cove, with the end result being two phenomenal pictures. Within one there appeared to be the form of a woman and in my imagination I thought of her as Peggy of the Wave.

Following that, I decided to paint a series of works called The Good Old Days of Peggy's Cove. Realizing nobody had ever painted the rescue of Peggy, I decided to complete such a work.

In the years that followed, my wife, April began creating poems and I too became interested in the process. It then became clear to me that I should write a poem to my wife. From that pleasant experience I was inspired to write a poem about Peggy of the Cove. That has since been put to music and has become a wonderful CD.

Why stop there, I thought. Why not write the story about Peggy, her rescue and life in the Cove. That, of course, resulted in this book, *Peggy of the Cove.*

Many of the stories in the book are true, some are gleaned from my own experiences as a boy living in Glen Margaret, just up the road from Peggy's Cove. My family, friends and neighbours living along St. Margaret's Bay related other stories to me. In the chapters School Days, Pranks and Unusual Happenings, The Little Yellow Shop, and other incidents like tragedies, are all true. Some stories in Life in the Cove and Uncle Willie's Blacksmith Shop are also true; others are from my vivid imagination.

Some think the name Peggy's Cove already existed and Peggy was named after it. Others believe Peggy's Cove came from the abbreviation of St. Margaret's Bay.

There are two versions of the legend of Peggy. One is by Bill deGarthe who describes Peggy as a young woman. The other is by Bruce Nunn who met Margaret Miller. She claims to be the great granddaughter of Peggy. You can read the account in his book, *"History with a Twist."* Margaret said the little girl who washed ashore was too young to remember her name. The family that took her in called her Peggy. Folks would say, "Let's go see Peggy of the Cove," thus derived Peggy's Cove.

Since there is question of which version is correct, I have created her story at the age of eight. She can't remember her past as a result of the tragedy. Reliving that horrific night through nightmares and dreams, she is able to write the details later in life. Slowly she begins to remember bits and pieces of her past.

There is so much to say about Peggy's life that a second book is in the works. It will answer many of Peggy's questions about her earlier life and take you through her adolescence.

I hope the story of Peggy of the Cove will fascinate you as much as it does me.

The Shipwreck

Excitement grew as we neared our journey's end, Nova Scotia! Joy filled every heart that contemplated a new adventurous beginning. It was a 'fair weather trip' according to the crew and even Captain Smith extolled the good fortune of gentle breezes, sunshine and ideal conditions during our long voyage.

The jolly crew entertained us with fascinating tales about the captain's seamanship. Oft times incredible odds challenged but he always conquered. Forty years of experience brought respect and confidence for this hearty but gentle seaman. Everybody anticipated a safe passage even though this was the season that storms could strike without warning.

Darkness came early in autumn but the sudden arrival of ominous clouds hastened the night. Gusty winds increased causing the waves to heave the ship, to the great discomfort of those aboard. Flying spray washed over the deck giving Captain Smith reason enough to order all passengers below. Though everyone was anxious to remain on deck, we knew he was thinking only of our safety.

Only a few suffered any discomfort on the voyage in fair weather, now motion sickness began taking its toll. Confined to the bunk area, the atmosphere became far from pleasant. The stench and sounds of those who were ill became unbearable. Our only light source, a lantern, began to swing back and forth as the ship rode the waves. Hypnotized by its swinging, my nausea intensified. I tried closing my eyes while remaining as still as possible. This was supposed to help one from getting sick, but it was to no avail. Of the dozen or so passengers in our area, only a few were blessed with iron stomachs. Soon, strong men and delicate ladies began asking for buckets. Even my parents looked strange and their faces had a weird, green tinge. They tried comforting me although they were having a worse time than I was. Big strong Mr. Johnson offered help and advice by saying that the main prevention for seasickness was to never think of food. That did it! I joined those that had used the buckets. After my third bout, I began to feel better. Now I know why sea folk always laugh about landlubbers getting seasick. "First yer afraid yer gonna die and then yer afraid ya won't," they joked.

Our problems, however, would get much worse. The wind roared and sheets of rain swept the sails and deck. Captain Smith ordered the sails lowered and trimmed as the storm intensified. Due to changing wind direction, tacking was required which made our progress slower still. Jim, the first mate, informed us that by tacking we would sail farther from the rocky coast and also have a better run with the wind. The Captain's intention was to make for St. Margaret's Bay and anchor just inside Shut-In Island to wait out the storm. We welcomed the news.

Though it was still dark, nobody slept. We would catch up on sleep once safely anchored. Jim explained that by just passing the entrance of St. Margaret's Bay, then coming about, it would be more favourable to enter the bay. Half an hour later the ship tacked again, heading for our sanctuary, Shut-In Island. That good news created sparks of joy distracting our minds from our miserably sick stomachs. The schooner rose on huge waves and then rushed down the crest as if surfing. Quickly she slowed as the bow plowed into the trough of the next wave. Passengers swayed back and forth like a swing while the ship fought that boiling sea. Plenty of action was happening on deck as the captain continually gave commands to the hardworking crew. It never ceased to amaze me how they worked all night without sleep and still had energy in reserve. They must have had nerves of steel. Maybe that's how they became known as 'iron men'. With increasing winds, the crew still had confidence in their skills, which encouraged us 'landlubbers'; the nickname seamen usually gave passengers who didn't have their 'sea legs' yet.

To the south, bright flashes of light jumped over the horizon and beamed through the small portholes. Fear of thunder and lightening brought more concerns. Even brave men can become cowards during thunderstorms. My mind flashed to terrible scenes as I saw and heard a number of passengers start to pray. Some didn't seem to have much use for God until now. I guess thunder and lightning, which was really getting close now, woke them up. Maybe the thought of dying without hope of going to heaven awakened their need of a Savior. Bright lightning, crashing thunder and pounding sea became constant. I thought this was the end. However, the sound of surf told us our refuge was closer, reviving fresh hope. Later in life I understood why people pray in a disaster. Rosa Hubley, who later became a close friend, always said, "There are no atheists when the ship is going down."

Only those familiar with the ways of the sea

understand how waves travel. Folks say every seventh wave is the big one. That is somewhat true but every twenty minutes or so there are very heavy seas and occasionally a rogue wave. Those are the ones to be frightened of. Well, by the feel of the rising boat, I figured we had encountered a rogue wave. It seemed like the schooner was climbing a mountain and when finally reaching the top, it stopped for a split second.

Suddenly, after the ship took a steep dive, everybody rolled forward trying to grab something for stability. Just as the ship was about to level off, there was a thunderous crash. We were sure lightning had struck. At the same time, an abnormal motion made it seem as though we were the ones moving, not the ship. All went flying forward, crashing into the bulkhead, causing screams and moans brought on by the sudden jolt of hitting solid walls.

Confusion immediately took command as the lantern sailed by and then shattered, leaving us in total darkness. Fortunately, the water suddenly washing into the hold extinguished the flames. It didn't take long to realize the boat had hit something solid and everyone was in dire trouble. Later I would learn that the ship had struck Halibut Rock. Water rushed in from all around creating need for a hasty escape. A crew member opened the hatch, commanding everybody on deck immediately. Fortunately he held a lantern that survived the crash. Movement was difficult for the injured. Fear grew instantly as we assessed our terrible plight. Some were crying while clinging to each other and yelling for help.

Captain Smith was missing which really added to the turmoil. The schooner dropped deeper into the ocean and filled with water in a matter of minutes. Waves rolled over the deck sweeping goods and people overboard. Some tried tying themselves to the masts but to no avail. By now it seemed certain all would be lost at sea. Just minutes earlier, everyone had hopes of reaching safety before the storm hit with full force. All that was gone now. Three men tried freeing a lifeboat but wind and waves battered with such force and frequency it was impossible. I hung onto my parents but became separated as another giant wave hit, washing us overboard. The water was so cold and furious and the thought of being buried in that cold dark sea was horrifying. When my head surfaced, I gasped for breath and thrashed about looking for mother and father. Screaming and crying didn't bring them. Where had they gone? Terror filled my heart as I searched for them. Suddenly my left hand hit something as I fumbled in the darkness trying to figure out what it was. I discovered it was a small barrel with a rope that was used as a floatation device when harpooning whales or tuna. How fortunate for me! I held on for dear life while still crying and yelling for my parents but there was no reply. Words cannot describe the fear that raced through my mind.

The local folks must have heard cries for help because small lights began to flicker along the rocky shore. Lights appeared to be going on and off when I realized the spray was flying so high it blocked my visibility. As another giant wave carried me to its top, I could see men hustling on shore trying to get close to the edge in hope of finding survivors. My body was freezing from the cold, and weak from being tossed about. It seemed impossible to reach safety but I kept praying and holding on. The pounding surf dead ahead threatened to crush my small body against those cold, hard cliffs. It appeared this merciless sea was going to do me in. As the distance from shore lessened, waves became steeper with a strong, boiling backwash that constantly changed direction. Keeping my grip became difficult not knowing which direction I would be thrown. The arrival of dawn revealed smooth rounded rocks not jagged and sharp like those nearby on my right. Would destiny wash me there to survive? At times it appeared I would miss the shore all together. Suddenly the changing surf swirled and tossed me onto smooth wet rock. However, the relief I felt was short lived. Another giant breaker approached, forcing local fishermen to safety. Again the backwash dragged me into the sea. Tired and worn, my exhausted body could fight no longer. Providentially, a calm spell offered moments of sweet relief. Another huge swell barreled toward me and I cried out as it lifted me high on its crest. Then I got the surprise of my life. It was as if an angel had guided me to higher ground where I lay safe from the vicious waves. Weak with exhaustion, I couldn't even move. Spray still splashed over me causing my mind to run wild. Would I again be dragged into that angry sea, swallowed and drowned? It seemed like an eternity as I lay there. Finally, I felt strong arms gently lifting me from that treacherous resting-place. Overwhelming joy filled my heart as this gallant man carried me safely to solid, dry land. With partially

Rescue of Peggy

opened eyes, I saw a lifeline of men holding a long rope; my rescuer tied to its end. Shouts of joy and congratulations rose from men, women and children who came in hopes of saving lives.

Now tears of relief washed away salt that covered my face. With my mind clearing, thoughts of my parents ran wild. I inquired with anxiety hoping that by some miracle they survived. The facial expressions of rescuers revealed the fateful answer. With sympathy they told me the sad news, all hands had been lost. I had been spared but how would I ever live without them?

My New Home

Rescuers wrapped me in dry, wool blankets. Oh, how I longed to be warm! Every inch of my body was shaking and shivering while my teeth chattered violently. The excited crowd rushed me to the nearest house, where upon opening the door, a blast of heat caused my cold face to sting with pain. I was taken into a bedroom and gently placed on the bed by the man who rescued me. He left as kind women quickly changed me into dry clothing. Getting out of those wet clothes didn't happen any too soon. My body was so blue from the cold it was shocking. The women helped me to the kitchen where a young man stoked a potbelly stove with wood. The heat turned the stovepipe almost red-hot. A cot placed beside the fire was a welcome sight. As I was propped with pillows, a gentle lady held a hot drink to my lips while others prepared soup. Another lady asked my name and where I was from. Fear set in as I realized my mind was blank and couldn't answer. Unable to hold them back, tears flowed while those present tried comforting me the best they knew how. After some time I settled enough to eat soup and crackers. It tasted so good and helped take away the cold feeling. The hot soup and warm fire finally warmed my shivering body. I became drowsy as my body warmed and relaxed. Now I realized how exhausted I felt and my eyelids became heavy. Before I knew it, my eyes closed as I fell into a deep sleep.

Later that morning, with sunshine peeking through the window, I woke in a daze. Was I dreaming? Where was I? What am I doing, here? Why is my body aching so? All these questions raced through my mind in a second. Then I remembered my horrible night. With loss of mother and father, I again cried, wondering how I would live or be happy without them. Where would I go, and what would I do? I was so scared!

My face was buried in the pillow so I didn't hear anyone come in. A warm smooth hand gently stroking my face and fingers combing through my hair startled me. A soft voice spoke saying, "It's ok, you are safe here. My name is Mary. What's yours?" As I turned and stared at Mary, I tried recalling my name but couldn't remember. Shocked, I searched wildly through the channels of my mind but nothing came. Finally I blurted out, while not being able to hold back the tears, "I still can't remember."

Mary said, "That's ok, I'm sure it'll come back to you. For now let's just call you Peggy so you will know we are speaking to you."

Mary just held me and neither of us said anything for some time. Finally I asked if my mother and father were found. Mary sadly shook her head while saying she was sorry.

"I understand the heartache you are going through," she said. "Just two years ago, my only little girl died from a fever. We have three boys, but all of us miss Elizabeth terribly. She was such a happy, joyful child." Mary's eyes were watery as she turned away while wiping them dry. Several minutes later she broke the silence. "While you were sleeping, a number of folks from the community met to decide which family would look after you. We made a decision. If it's fine with you, my family and I would love to have you live with us. I haven't been able to change Elizabeth's room. It's just like it was before she died. It would become yours. She was your size so her clothes will fit you perfectly. Matter of fact, you have her nightgown on now. See how nicely it fits."

Mary's voice was so kind she reminded me of my mother. Even though I was only young, I knew I needed someone to take care of me. Her face told me she was longing for a reply. Not able to contain myself any longer, I said, "Yes!" while we both embraced. Tears of joy and sorrow flowed, knowing we each had needs we didn't think could ever be filled. Neither of us could replace our loss but this was the next best thing. It felt so good to be hugged and wanted so soon. I'll never, ever forget that moment. I have been greatly blessed and am very thankful.

Mary placed clothes on the bed, telling me they were mine to keep. After I was dressed, a meal would be ready for me downstairs. Apparently someone had carried me upstairs, after falling asleep. By now it was almost dinnertime. As I crawled out of bed, my muscles ached with every move. I had never felt like this before. My battle with the sea was the cause. After dressing, Mary came in and held my hand as we went downstairs to the dining room. A number of ladies were present. I couldn't remember their names. They stared, which made me feel uncomfortable. Mary helped by getting them busy doing things and giving me my meal. She told me we would go to her place after I ate.

Eating with strangers was difficult, so after a little while, Mary brought a coat and shoes. I was shy and even though most of the women were in the kitchen, I was scared. They must have been talking about me in the other room because sometimes they whispered. One woman spelled a few words. I thought they must have been saying something they didn't want me to hear. Mary sensed my uneasiness and got me ready quietly. She seemed to read my mind.

Going outside was another surprise. This land was so different from anything I seemed to remember. The wind had changed direction, bringing warm air from the northwest. I could still hear pounding waves but nothing like it was earlier. I sensed a quiet atmosphere; the community grieved the tragic loss of life and I was obviously on their minds. Brightly coloured houses perched on hilltops glowed in the midday sun. Seagulls soared above fishing boats and sheds, looking for a free meal. Fishermen were gathering salt cod from the drying racks. Those close by gave a nod and a small wave as if to say "Good day, ladies." Children coming from school looked at us curiously then slowly headed in all directions. Mary pointed out some of the children while giving their names but there were too many for me to remember. I noticed a lot of chicken houses, a number of cows, oxen and a couple of horses. I liked horses, that much I knew. There weren't many fields, mainly rocks with grass scattered between. I wondered how on earth the animals got enough grass.

I asked, "Is it always this warm?"

"No. This is what we call Indian Summer," she explained. "During the fall we experience a warm period for a week or so." The sun was warm but I could feel coolness in the wind. As we turned off the road onto a path, Mary said, "This is our home." It looked like a nice place.

Entering the main door, I stopped while taking in my new surroundings. It was quite different from what

I expected. It was a simple home but neat and clean with everything in its place. Mary took me through the living room, dining room and then to the kitchen. A pot of stew simmering on the stove filled the house with a wonderful smell. No sooner had we reached the kitchen when three boys raced in. Oh my! More introductions, I thought. James was the oldest, next Peter and the youngest was Joseph or Joe, as they called him. He appeared to be my age while I knew the other two were older. It was difficult knowing what to say to each other. I could tell they felt the pain of my loss and no doubt were reminded of losing their sister. Mary said nothing about my memory loss in front of them. She protected me from embarrassment by simply introducing me as Peggy. I was sure they all knew about the night before but I still appreciated her kindness. Just then a stately man came through the door. Mary told me this was her husband, John. I was shocked when I looked into his face! He was the one at the end of the rope who rescued me! Even though I was exhausted, I did get a chance to look into his sympathetic face as he put me on the bed. Nobody, not even Mary, mentioned that John was the one who risked his life to save mine. We bonded immediately.

Mary told everyone to help themselves to dinner, while she took care of me. We went upstairs to what would be my room. It was small but bright, and again, everything was in its place. A bureau with two dolls sitting on top caught my eye immediately. Holding them gave me a sense of belonging. A big chest sat in the corner by the window. I wondered what was in it. The bed was nicely made and a quilt of brightly coloured flowers gave a cheery atmosphere. Floral wallpaper matched the bedspread. A commode with a large porcelain pitcher and wash basin was on the other side of the bed. Mary told me the chamber pot was inside. On the door hung dresses and nightclothes nicely arranged. A large hooked mat covered the floor near the bed. That would be warm and soft on the feet. A nice little rocking chair looked inviting as well.

I sat on the edge of the bed, not knowing quite what to do next. Mary asked if I liked it. Of course I answered yes. She then sat down while putting her arm around me. She told me she realized how difficult and strange this must be, but the family would do everything they could to make me happy and feel welcome.

As we sat quietly, I couldn't help saying that I missed my mother and father. I tried not to cry, but tears ran down my cheeks anyway. Mary said she understood and took me to the rocking chair and rocked me for a long time. Neither of us said anything, we just rocked. I tried imagining the warmth I felt was from my mother and that helped take away the pain. Although I didn't go into a deep sleep, I did get a little rest. A door downstairs banged shut as John and the boys left after dinner. It startled me and woke me from my slumber. Mary said she had to go downstairs, clean up, do a few errands and then prepare supper. She said I could come along or stay in my room. I went with her, not wanting to be alone.

As we turned to go downstairs, I took a glimpse out the window. I could see a few men along the cliffs. Later I learned they were looking for bodies. Nobody was found because the wind had changed direction, now blowing everything out to sea. Only a few planks that were hardly recognizable were found.

Mary cleared the dining room table, put away the leftovers and washed the dishes. She kept the fire going for hot water and to finish baking beans for supper. The smell was wonderful, as was the sound of crackling wood, and the whistling teakettle. Humming while working, she occasionally looked my way with a little smile that gave me a welcome feeling. I just sat in the rocking chair by the window looking out, wondering why this was happening to me!

My mind questioned why God let me live, while my parents were lost. I thought that He would protect us in times of danger so where was He last night? Was I a bad girl and now God was punishing me? If so, what did I do? Not being able to find answers, I finally asked Mary if God was punishing me? She immediately stopped her work, brought over a chair and sat down beside me.

"No, Peggy, you are not a bad girl," she assured me. "We do not live in a perfect world so sometimes bad things happen to good people. Just like often good things happen to people who do bad things." Mary said she had the same questions when Elizabeth died. "After Elizabeth was born, the doctor said I wouldn't be able to have any more children. I did mind but I had three boys and at least one girl. Then I lost my only daughter. I was terribly sorrowful. It just didn't make sense.

"Now let's talk about you, your family and God. I believe God hasn't taken away all the results of sin yet. Some day, He will. Jesus will come again to take those that love Him to heaven. We will then be with our families forever, if they too accept Him as their Savior. Forever is a long time and may seem like it will never come, but as you get older, time will go by so quickly, you will wonder where it went. We don't know why you are the only one alive, but here you are. In heaven, we can ask God why He permitted unhappy things to come into our lives. Someone once said that when we are in heaven and look back, we would not change the way God had led us. I guess we won't know if that will be our case until we get there. In the meantime, you can be thankful that you have a safe, happy home. We will do everything possible to make you welcome and be part of our family even if we aren't your real mother, father and brothers."

It didn't make a lot of sense, but Mary's confidence in God helped. She did have a kind voice and her face showed lots of love. It still was a scary thought though, not having my parents and being with a strange family and community. I only hoped she was right and that I would be happy again. How quickly my life has changed! I continued looking through the window and wondering.

Mary was putting the final touches on a dress, which she needed to deliver to Mrs. Crooks. As it turned out, Mary was a seamstress, which helped earn extra money. I really didn't want to go out or stay alone. She said it was such a lovely day we should enjoy the warm sunshine while it lasted, so I went along with her.

The walk to Mrs. Crooks' house was a short distance. Since the door was open, she saw us coming and welcomed us in. Mary just said, "This is Peggy." I was glad she didn't go into any further details about me. Mrs. Crooks smiled and said, "Hello, Peggy, it's so nice to meet you. My, you are a pretty little girl. Do come in."

We stepped inside while Mrs. Crooks went right to the kitchen and returned with warm cookies. "Here Peggy, help yourself, I just took these out of the oven." I couldn't resist since the aroma throughout the house was of freshly baked cookies. They melted in my mouth and were so good I could have eaten all of them, but knew it wasn't polite. While I was enjoying the treat, Mrs. Crooks put on the dress and complimented Mary on how wonderfully it fit. There was a sparkle in Mary's eyes as she graciously accepted the praise. Mrs. Crooks

Mary's Favorite Path

told me Mary was the best seamstress around. "There isn't anything she can't do when it comes to sewing." After receiving payment, they chatted a few minutes then Mary said it was time to go. I thanked Mrs. Crooks again for the cookies. She said I was most welcome and to come visit any time I wanted. She loved company, especially children. After tasting those cookies, I was sure I would visit often.

Getting outside and absorbing the sunshine was healing. It seemed to help my aching body, both physically and mentally. I was hurting so badly for my parents. Mary understood and tried getting my mind on pleasant things like the brilliant crimson of the blueberry and huckleberry bushes. She described how the frost turned them to the most beautiful colours, which were even more glorious early in the morning when wet with dew. She told how early sunrays created bright reds with deep shadows while mist rising from small ponds gently swirled upward evaporating into thin air. "Those are moments you will never forget," she explained. "Tomorrow, if it's sunny, I will wake you early so we can walk through the hills and you can see for yourself. You'll love it!"

When we arrived at the house, Joe asked if I wanted to help dig carrots. The boys had three rows to pull before they could play.

I said, "I guess so, but I don't know how to do it."

"Don't worry about that," they said, "We'll show you. We have to put away our books, get some knives and off we'll go."

I dreaded the thought that maybe they would ask about my past. Mary must have said something when they went inside because nobody asked a question about my family or where I came from.

James came out first. He was a strong looking

teenager who resembled his dad. As we walked, he told me this was his last year in school. No doubt he would go fishing like most others his age. He directed me around the corner of the house. There was a bright, red wheelbarrow.

"Jump in while I take you for a ride," he said. I wasn't sure about that, but awkwardly climbed in not wanting to act like a scaredy cat. He took off running before I knew what was happening. It was the bumpiest ride you could imagine but lots of fun.

By now Peter and Joe were chasing behind while yelling, "Faster James, faster." It's a good thing their knives were in cases or had they fallen they might have stabbed themselves. Around rocks, over little hilly spots and finally reaching the garden, we came to a sudden stop.

"How'd you like that?" they asked. "Hope we didn't scare you."

"Pretty good," I said, while getting out and dusting myself off. "It was so bumpy my teeth clattered."

For a minute, I did hold my breath and hung on for fear of bouncing out but didn't want to let them know. I pretended to be as brave as they were. Then they told me how Elizabeth loved wheelbarrow rides and would scream for them to go as fast as they could. Now it made sense why the other two kept telling James to go faster. At first I thought they might be trying to scare me but was happy to know they were just trying to give me a joy ride.

James took a shovel and loosened the ground while Peter and Joe pulled carrots and cut off the tops. I started pulling too but didn't do any cutting. They must have used knives a lot because they didn't cut themselves once. It was amazing how fast they worked. About an hour later, they finished pulling the three rows of carrots, and headed back to the house with the wheelbarrow full. No ride for me this time!

They used buckets to carry the carrots down the cellar, then buried them in a large box of sand. James told me that sand, along with coolness, preserved them for months. Mary had many bottles of vegetables and fruit preserved for the winter. Red beets, orange carrots, green and yellow beans, blueberries, rhubarb, applesauce, peas, and a variety of jams arranged neatly in rows made my mouth water just looking at them. Peter said by next summer, the shelves would be bare.

As there was an hour before supper, the boys went down to the wharf to try their hand at fishing. They invited me but I wasn't interested, so I went back into the house with Mary.

"Did James take you for a wheelbarrow ride," she asked?

"Yes, how did you know?"

"Well, I thought he would since Elizabeth liked it so much. They were very close. It was hard to believe a brother and sister could get along as well as those two did. Of the three boys, James took her death the hardest. We noticed a big change in his behavior. He became withdrawn, quiet, and often went for long walks along the shore. Having you here may put spark back into his life."

Mary asked if I would set the table. She showed me where everything was and how to place the setting. She then told me where each person sat, not that it made any difference to where the dishes were placed. She sat on the side closest to the kitchen; John was on her right, Joe on the left end, James across from his mother and Peter across from his father. She said nothing about where Elizabeth sat, so I guessed it was the end closest to John, which would now be my place. It was a strange feeling. I hoped they wouldn't compare me to Elizabeth.

Mary took the crock of beans from the oven and placed them on the stove where they would stay warm but not bake. She popped two apple pies into the oven saying it was going to be close timing to have them ready for supper. It wasn't long before the wonderful aroma wafted from the oven to my nose. Oh, how it made my mouth water! There was something familiar about the aroma of apple pie. She then placed a big frying pan full of cut potatoes on the hottest spot of the stove. She instructed me to turn them occasionally until they were a crispy brown on the outside. She said I must be a natural cook since they were fried just right. Of course she kept her eye on them as they were frying. Then they were placed beside the beans to keep warm as well.

By the time John and the boys arrived, everything was ready. They got washed up and sat around the table. Without saying a word, they all bowed their heads while John said grace. I just followed along not knowing quite what I was supposed to do. All the food was on the table as everyone reached for something. Whatever was nearest was what each one put on their plate, then passed it on to the next. Since I was close to John, he just put a helping on my plate. Everyone else took as much as they wanted. John said if that wasn't enough, I could have more, but save room for the apple pie. He didn't have to tell me because I was already thinking about that.

Everyone talked while they ate. It was a pleasant time. They talked about what they did throughout the day, but nobody mentioned the shipwreck or me. After eating, and the supper tasted very good, everyone took their own dishes to the sink, rinsed them off, and stacked them. Nobody told them what to do they just did it. It must have been their routine. I was at a loss about what to do, but Mary took my dishes that night. They sat around and talked a while before doing the final chores of the day. It was all new and strange but a pleasant time.

John and the two older boys went to the barn to feed and milk the cow. They took care of the horse, too. Joe's chore was to look after the chickens, gather the eggs and bring in wood. He invited me along, and Mary encouraged me to go. They had a lot of hens. When we entered the hen house, a large rooster charged me with ruffled feathers, ready to attack. Joe chased it outside and told me not to be afraid of any rooster. He filled the water and feed troughs. We then collected over a dozen eggs. He showed me a trick; demonstrating how strong eggshells were by placing one egg end to end between the palm of his hands and squeezing with all his might. He even bent over, placed his hands between his knees and squeezed with both knees and hands but could not break it. He told me to try and I couldn't break it either. I was amazed, as I didn't remember having seen that before. Joe reminisced about the time there was only one egg a certain evening so he put it in his coat pocket. It was winter and a lot of snow had fallen. He and Peter had been playing in the snow, actually more like wrestling. He forgot all about the egg. He remembered as he took off his coat, and to his surprise, it hadn't even cracked. Another time he wasn't that fortunate. Again, that particular night, there was only one egg. The next morning was cold but the kids played outside before going to school. At school he reached inside his pocket, or tried to but it was frozen shut. The egg had broken and was frozen. There had been an awful mess of egg on his hand when he reached inside after it had thawed.

We then carried some wood inside. Joe took such a big load, mine looked tiny in comparison. Mary called Joe's a lazy man's load. Joe said, "Can you imagine a load this size being a lazy man's load." I think he was trying to impress me.

Mary called it by that name, because lazy people didn't want to make too many trips. She explained, "Last winter he brought the biggest load ever. He held a long piece of wood in one hand, which kept the wood from falling, piled as much as he could and then held the top of the stick with his other hand. The weight was so heavy he could barely walk. Coming across the floor with snow-covered boots proved to be a disaster. Snow stuck on the heel was like greased lightning and caused his left foot to fly forward. Down he went with a crash, wood covering him as he fell backwards. Fortunately, the only thing hurt was his pride. That was the last time he brought a load too big to handle."

Joe had a little grin on his face, taking the ribbing with a sense of humour. "Yeah, but I could fill the wood box with three loads instead of the usual five or six. Just think of all the time I saved." We all chuckled.

We finished Joe's chores before the others. He started his homework so I looked at the textbooks to see what they were like. Shortly after, the others came in with milk. They smelled like a barn. I turned up my nose. They laughed when I plugged it. "You'll get used to that smell." I didn't know how. Peter and James then did their homework, while John read and Mary did some knitting. She noticed me watching her and asked if I knew how to knit.

"No."

"Would you like to learn?"

"Yes!"

"Come here and I'll teach you." Handling needles

was awkward, but soon I managed to get a few stitches that actually looked pretty good.

After a time, I felt sleepy. Mary helped get me ready for bed and read a story to me. Getting to sleep wasn't easy that night or for many nights later. It was quite some time before I didn't cry for mother and father, especially at bedtime. Mary read every night and sometimes I would fall asleep before she finished. I really liked her a lot. She knew just what I needed.

As days turned into weeks, adjusting to a new family, school, friends and way of life began to bring security and a feeling of belonging. The love Mary and John showed for each other, their boys and me, would melt the coldest of hearts. Joy, along with security, abounded, as I became part of the family and community.

Days passed quickly bringing cold, north winds, which caused temperatures to dip below freezing. By late November snow flurries arrived and before Christmas the ground was covered with a blanket of beautiful white snow. Young people took advantage of winter by sleigh riding or skating on the ponds. Hills at the Cove weren't high or long but we had barrels of fun anyway. For big thrills, the place to go was Fraser's. Riding down that hill was scary as the sleigh traveled at tremendous speed. Getting there was the problem because of the distance but the effort was well worth it. Whenever John took the horse and sleigh up to the Glen, and it wasn't a school day, we would coax him into dropping us off so we could slide. It didn't happen often, but when it did, what a thrill! Those nights we slept like babies after making numerous trips up and down the hill.

Another enjoyable experience was riding the sleigh loaded with wood, pulled by oxen or a horse. Most families owned tree lots deep in the woods. Two trips a day were about all the men folk could manage due to the distance. The scenery was breathtaking with snow-laden boughs bending to their limit. Snow absorbs sound creating silence except for the bells clanging on the animals or cries from blue jays or crows that didn't go south. Occasionally a rabbit hopped into the deep woods out of view, hiding from danger. Memories from those days are etched deep in my mind. How beautiful this simple lifestyle was.

Temperatures dropped below zero on two or three spells during winter, making outdoor activities unimaginable. The contest on freezing mornings was to jump from a snugly warm bed to get dressed before you froze to death. Brave John made it easy for us. He was up at five daily, making a fire in both kitchen and living room stoves. Downstairs was toasty warm by breakfast. I was always grateful.

Our poor neighbour, little Johnny thought he'd outsmart the cold. He took his long johns and other clothes to the living room and warned everyone to stay out while he changed. Their stove was roaring hot and had sharp corners. "Oh how nice and warm this is changing here," he thought, "I am so smart." As he leaned over to put on his long johns, his rear end hit the corner of the extremely hot stove. Everyone in the house heard the yelp as he jumped and danced holding his burned spot. What a predicament! He wanted to sit in water to soothe the pain but couldn't. "This is too embarrassing," he thought, "Whatever shall I do?" Quickly dressing, he rushed to his mother for advice. She provided ointment but the burn was too severe and that day he stayed home from school.

March brought warmer air and daylight hours increased considerably. Spring was just around the corner and Easter with it. Mary said I could bring my new friends over and she'd help us colour eggs. The afternoon was filled with laughter as we later decided to put faces on them. We tried drawing each other and Joe, Peter and James too. Nobody could guess whose picture it was so we wrote their initials on them. We thought they would be surprised Easter morning. Hats were set out Saturday night, in the hopes of lots of treats. James didn't, he thought he was too grown up. Mary put his things in a bag with his name on it. He didn't refuse. Easter and Christmas were times the church was full. Seems everyone thought about religious things at those times.

Catching Pollock

Every spring young pollock migrate to bays and coves along Nova Scotia's coastline. The Cove is one of their yearly spots to visit. James, Peter and Joe were going fishing and invited me to come along. "Everyone will be there," they said. Sure enough, the wharves and boats were lined with kids of all ages. Even the teenagers got excited. Pollock take almost any bait so it's not a matter of success but how many one will catch. That was the contest, who could catch the most.

Evening is the best time to catch them especially if it's calm. We pronounced "calm" like "cam" so the teacher always tried to correct our mispronunciation. She never succeeded. Jubilant shouts or laughter echoed as someone yelled, "I got another one." It would be difficult to find anyone who didn't have fond memories of pollock fishing at the Cove. Cats too, gathered, looking for a meal of fresh fish. No cat ever went to bed hungry when the pollock were running.

After the pollock fishing season wound down, groups of kids and, many times, adults, gathered at the spot they called, "The Dancing Rock." It was a large, flat area close to the water but up high enough to be safe unless stormy weather arrived. It was a favourite spot for picnics too. One day I decided to explore that spot and met a girl named Sally. She and I saw a couple, Charles and Bernice, disappearing over the brow of the cliffs to "The Dancing Rock."

Sally said, "I think they are going there to kiss. Let's go sneak up on them and see." We snickered and quietly walked along the rocks to where we could peek down on them. They were holding hands and talking but finally Charles leaned over and gave Bernice a peck on the cheek. They jumped when we startled them by our giggles.

"Hey, girls, what do you think you're doing," Charles fumed. He came running after us, so we ran as fast as our little legs would carry us. Fortunately he didn't come far but went back to Bernice. Then they left and went over to one of my favourite spots to watch the waves. It's called "The Devil's Corner." The rocks are high and steep, almost straight down. A sharp edge causes waves to break and foam as they try to round the corner. There is a ledge near the bottom of the cliff and boys love to show their bravery as they edge their way out. Often high seas make access to the ledge impossible. Calmer waters challenge some boys who descend the cliff ignoring almost certain disaster. It terrifies me. I wish they wouldn't do it. Whenever anyone suggests going on it, I leave. It brings to mind many sad memories.

The Devil's Corner

Hector

My first day with Mary included a visit to the store. I waited outside on a bench soaking up the sun, when I heard an awful screeching of a seagull. Turning in the direction of the noise, I saw the poor bird with its leg tangled in a net that was drying on the rocks. The gull was getting a free meal of starfish and crabs that were scattered in the net when it got its leg caught. I quickly went to help set it free. As I came near, it squawked even more and tried to fly away. I was afraid it was going to pull its leg off. Watching for a minute or two, not knowing what exactly to do, it finally settled down, and I hoped I wouldn't hurt the poor thing. I bent down to untangle its leg but it hopped and cocked its head one way and then another with wings outstretched. As I reached for the leg, it jumped back as it screeched again. The gull began pecking at me, however the bites really didn't hurt. They were more like warnings saying; "Don't you hurt me now." With both of us becoming friendly, it soon let me remove the net. When free, it just stood there for a minute, head turning one way and then another with its beady eye looking me over as if to say, "You aren't so bad after all, thank you for setting me free, wanna be friends?" Then it quietly opened its wings and flew above me circling overhead. Strange cries came from its beak as if it was telling the whole Cove what just happened. I felt good inside knowing I was able to help it and smiled at the excitement it caused. By now other gulls gathered. I wished I could understand their language because of all the squealing and squawking going on. It would be interesting to know what they said.

Hector

Just then Mary came along; asking what all the noise was about. I told her the whole story. We both smiled as I pointed to the gull I had just rescued. It was still gliding overhead, following us as we headed home. I knew it by the shape and placement of a red mark on its beak. The rest of the gulls went back to whatever they were doing, but this one stayed close by all the way home. Mary asked if I would like to give it a crust of bread as the gull perched on the roof. "Oh yes, may I?" I replied.

"Of course you may, you stay here and I'll get the crust." Mary told me to break it into pieces and throw it far as I could so the gull wouldn't be afraid to get it. Sure enough, soon as the bread left my hand, the gull took flight, swooped down and grabbed it. In a short time, the whole crust was gone. I was so pleased but wondered if he would be back again as it flew to join the others.

Being so happy with the gull experience, I didn't notice the boys coming up the path. "Hi, Peggy," they said, "what are you looking at?" Telling them of the gull rescue was exciting, which took away my fear of talking. They were sure the gull would become a pet because others fed them to the point where they would take food from a person's hand. It was my hope this gull would return for a meal, and we could become friends. Mary told John about my experience with the sea gull. He said no doubt it would be back. I hoped so.

Sure enough, my flying friend arrived early the next morning, perched on the rooftop waiting for me to wake. John saw it all as he was up early doing chores in the barn. Mary gave me another crust of bread. Just as soon as the door opened, he took flight, circling until I threw the bread. With wings in diving position, he swooped down, landed and in a gulp or two, the whole piece was devoured. It was so funny watching him. How could a bird swallow without chewing?

At that moment, giving him a name struck me like lightning. I wondered what name would be best for a seagull? Miss Smith was talking in school about a ship named 'Hector,' to the higher grades. I liked what I heard, including the sound. I had Mary look it up in the dictionary. My favorite meanings were 'to tease, to threaten, bully or to dominate in a blustering way.' When I tried to rescue Hector, all meanings fit exactly except tease. He wanted to be set free but didn't know I was there to help. As you already know, I was shocked, amused and startled by his bravery. Yes, Hector was the best name for my new friend.

As time passed, the bonding between us grew

beyond my wildest dreams. I had no idea birds related to kids so well. Every morning he was awake early, looking for a free handout and circling overhead as I made my way to school or down to the wharf. It was as if he was watching over me. Other kids could get close to him, but weren't able to feed him with their hands like I could. Many times Hector made loud calls with quite a variety of sounds. He brought joy into my life. I just wished I could fly too. Just think of the fun that we could have gliding on wind currents caused by the updraft from rocky cliffs. I would love diving at fast speeds as we swooped low and then up and away to great heights. Skimming over calm waters or wave crests would be such a thrill, I'd never forget. I thought about it so much, one night I actually dreamed I was flying! It was the time of my life, but what a disappointment when I woke up.

If we went fishing, Hector was always watching. Sometimes he would land on the bow of the boat as we rowed to our favourite fishing spot. He tried to steal fish if they were the size he could eat. Sometimes he was successful. Other gulls flocked around the boat, but Hector made funny gestures and noises, scaring them away if they got too close. He was boss of the flock.

My first spring brought another surprise. Hector had a girlfriend. He still came every morning wanting food but gave his mate first choice of the meal. He was such a gentleman then but not always! Now I had to name her, too. For some strange reason, 'Becky' popped into my head. So, 'Becky' it would be without a second thought. There was neither rhyme nor reason for my choice, it just seemed right. They were always together for a few weeks, but later in the spring, only one showed up at a time. No doubt they were taking turns sitting on their nest.

Hector and his mate flew in for food but didn't stay long. Soon it would be baby time. They were so cute though, sometimes standing on a rock side by side, making funny motions and strange sounds. Other times they appeared to be playing tag while flying, dodging and doing all sorts of acrobats.

John said, "Isn't love grand, take a lesson from the birds." He told the boys when they got older to treat their lady friends like Hector treated his. Provide, protect and love. Even though I was young, it sounded good to me.

School Days

My first week with Mary was spent in emotional healing and getting to know the family. Adjusting was easier for them than it was for me, especially since I was an only child. That I did remember. Dealing with boys in a family became more of a challenge than I had imagined. Peter and Joe had no idea about the sensitivities of girls. James did a much better job, but boys in general need to walk in our shoes for a week, sometimes longer. The family introduced me to a few children who were friendly and kind. Acceptance into the community gave me a sense of belonging.

"Peggy, I think you should begin school next week," Mary suggested. "We can visit Miss Smith Friday after school to decide what grade you should be in."

"Yes, I know you're right," I said, "Still I'm nervous about getting started."

Friday afternoon arrived quickly. Mary waited until every student went home before leaving for the school. I was more than a little anxious but holding her warm hand calmed me.

Miss Smith shook my hand while saying, "Welcome Peggy, please have a seat. I've heard a lot about you from Sally and Mary's boys. The other students are looking forward to meeting you so I'm sure you will feel welcome. Do you have any questions before we start?"

"No, I don't think so."

"Well, if at any time you need anything explained, feel free to ask. I'm going to go over a number of questions to find what grade I think you should be in. Don't be afraid to answer or if you don't know, just tell me."

She went over arithmetic, reading, spelling, printing and a lot of other questions. At first I knew most of the right answers, but as time went on, I didn't.

"Peggy, you may have noticed the questions became more difficult. That's because they are for a higher grade. I would have been greatly surprised if you knew the correct answers."

After talking to Mary, Miss Smith thought I would be most comfortable in grade three. She told me that I might go back if it was too hard or ahead to grade four if I found it too easy.

So it was settled, Monday morning would be my first day of school! There were four girls and three boys in grade three with me.

Peggy's Cove School

"I thought you would like sharing a desk with Sally since you already know her, is that all right with you Peggy?"

"Yes, thank you, I would like that very much."

Monday morning arrived all too soon. My nerves were jangled. I wondered if the children would tease and make fun of me or ask about my past. How would they react if I couldn't remember their names because I certainly didn't know many of them? Mary must have seen fear on my face, because she told me to think of the new friends I would make and the fun I would have with Sally.

Sally was nice to me I had to agree. She was bigger and stronger even though we were in the same grade. She acted tough like the boys. Being with her gave me a feeling of safety. James, Peter and Joe seemed excited about my going with them, but I didn't know why.

"Come on, Peggy," they urged, "Hurry, we can play tag or hide-and-seek before school starts."

The boys did hurry, so not wanting to show up alone, I had to keep up with them. They told me the names of a number of boys and girls and I tried to keep the right name with the right face. It wasn't easy, especially as there were a lot of them. They all knew who I was. Sally arrived just in time.

"Hi Peggy," she said, "want to join us in a game of hopscotch."

I accepted, feeling comfortable with her. They explained the rules, which seemed easy but throwing the flat rock in the right space was a different story. The first few blocks were easy to reach, but jumping over spaces with stones was something else, especially with four players. I just started getting the hang of it when we heard the clanging of a bell. It was the call to go inside.

After getting settled, Miss Smith said, "Good morning everyone, this is a special day. As you all know, Peggy is new here. I hope you give her the typical Nova Scotia welcome."

Oh my, I thought, they are all looking at me. Will I turn beet red? I could feel my face getting warm. Miss Smith must have seen my predicament because she instantly said, "I want each of you to take a small piece of paper and write your name on it. Joe, will you take these pins and give them out? I want each of you to pin your name on your collar and leave it there all day. That will help Peggy know who you are and remember your name."

Phew, that was a relief, I felt my face cooling as the attention was taken off me.

"I still want you to say your name," Miss Smith insisted, "We'll start with you Peter, and go in order right to the last student."

One girl, Blanch seemed to be annoyed for some reason. I could tell by the tone of her voice. I wondered what I had done that caused her to act as if she didn't like me.

Miss Smith must have noticed because it was only after her introduction, that she made a comment. "I'm sure Peggy will be a good friend to all."

Miss Smith then gave each grade their assignment. I was relieved to have Sally beside me because a number of kids seemed to be paying more attention to me than their work. I wondered why they were staring instead of doing schoolwork. Time crawled by, but recess did finally arrive, giving us a chance to continue our game of hopscotch.

Nearby, Blanch was talking to a small group of girls who giggled and looked my way. It appeared they were making fun of me but I didn't say anything to Sally. All went well the rest of the day until school was out. The teacher asked Sally to stay for a few minutes. As we had planned to spend time together after school, I told Sally I would wait outside. I thought practicing hopscotch might be a good idea. As I was enjoying myself, Blanch and two other girls came over.

"We want to play, so would you move?" Blanch asked rudely.

"No, I was here first, but you may join me if you like," I replied as polite as I could muster up. I could sense a conflict arising.

"Forget it!" She turned to walk away, but then stopped. "Hey, Peggy, by the way, what's your last name?"

I was horrified standing there not knowing what to say as my face turned red as a beet. I was deeply hurt too.

"What's the matter, don't you know?" she said, as they all laughed.

Why were they doing this to me? What had I done to deserve this, I wondered? Just then Sally arrived and saw my horrified look while the three girls continued laughing.

"What's so funny?"

"Peggy doesn't know her last name," Blanch snickered.

The look on Sally's face changed from inquisitive to anger. "And you think that's funny?" she replied with a grim look on her face. "Well, see if you think this is funny." And with that she pushed Blanch, who tried to gain her balance, but not in time. As she went backwards, her heel caught on a rock, causing her to fall, and books went flying. Her friends helped her up, instantly plugging their noses. She had landed in 'doggie doo'. The smell was far from pleasant.

"You just wait till I tell on you," fumed Blanch, "you're going to be in big trouble."

"Yeah, well you leave Peggy alone or else. Do you hear me?"

Nearby, kids quickly gathered, thinking a fight was about to erupt. Seeing what happened, they pointed to Blanch's backside saying, "Yuk, look at that," and burst out laughing.

"Get her back," Michael yelled, wanting to see a good fight between two girls, but Blanch stomped off toward home, in a hurry to get changed no doubt.

"You shouldn't have done that Sally, but I appreciate you standing up for me."

"That's OK. Blanch thinks she's a queen and needs to be put in her place. If she ever bothers you again, you just let me know. I'll take care of her."

"You are going to be in trouble."

"Don't you worry about me, I can take care of myself," Sally assured me. I still thought we would hear more about the incident.

With that, we headed to my place; ready to play and feed Hector who always wanted a free meal.

On our way to my place, Sally wanted to get candy from the store. It was handy having it so close. Then again, each village had a post office, church, school and general store as a convenience.

"How do you like Miss Smith," Sally asked.

"Oh! I think she's just a wonderful person, don't you?"

"Yes, I agree, but I don't like homework. I'm glad she doesn't give us too much. The higher grades get plenty though. I don't look forward to that. I guess we're lucky though. Getting teachers to locate in isolated communities is no easy task. Occasionally trustees have to take whoever is available or do without a teacher. We are fortunate to have Miss Smith; some schools have pretty bad teachers. At least that's what I heard Mother and Dad say."

"Tell me, Sally, has the school always been the same and who decides what is done?."

"Trustees, they make all the decisions. They even choose the colour to paint the school. It's been different over the years. Brown just happens to be the colour now. You saw the potbelly stove?"

"Yes, what about it?"

"Well, Eddie Morash gets up early and starts a coal fire, making it comfortable for us on those cold winter days. Coal is used because trees don't have the soil to grow very big around the Cove, and due to strong, salty winds and rocky terrain. Wood, mostly from Ingramport, comes by boat, like many supplies."

"When did they start playing card games at the school," I asked.

"Oh, ever since I can remember. Nearly all the adults go but not on a weekly basis. Did you know Mary and John don't play cards because of their religious beliefs?"

"Mary hadn't said anything about card games to me yet. Maybe she will if I mention it."

We continued chatting on the way to my place. Hector flew past giving his usual calls. "Don't you wish you could understand gull talk?"

"Oh! Peggy, you are so funny," Sally laughed. "I suppose it would be rather wonderful."

"Tell me something, Sally, do you get bored with school?"

"Oh, yeah, especially in the spring when it gets warm! As the school overlooks the Cove, it's tempting to watch boats come and go throughout the day. Spotting visitors is easy since we recognize every boat and owner in the cove. The clock seems to crawl while waiting for recess, when we rush to see any strange vessels or the patrol boat. Whenever it comes to the Cove, someone is sure to yell, "Here comes the patrol boat." We always thought the skipper, Captain Jeff Williams, made excuses to stop. He courted Olive Norton, which later led to a happy union in marriage."

Since Christmas was just around the corner, preparation for the annual school concert took priority. With exams over, we could concentrate on skits, songs and recitals. The main play was *Cinderella*. They chose me to be the main character. I was nervous, but happy for the opportunity to act. My shyness didn't affect acting in the least. What a relief! As the curtain closed, the audience applauded long and loud.

Lastly, Santa, who called our names, gave out gifts. We had exchanged names earlier and guess whose name I got. Blanch, of all people, not one of my favourite schoolmates.

Mary thought it providential, "Perhaps this would patch your differences, presenting an opportunity to become good friends."

Yuck, I thought, could I ever like her? Mary had inquired as to what Blanch might like and discovered she loved dolls. As she had never owned a special one, Mary put extra work into creating a beautiful rag doll. I helped but she did most of the work. When Blanch's name was called, I watched out of the corner of my eye to see her reaction. The surprised look on her face and the big smile while holding the doll close indicated we had made the right choice. Maybe she was touched because she wiped her eyes while her mother gave her a hug.

My gift from Roger was a beautiful red scarf. Red is my favourite colour. I couldn't wait and wrapped it around my neck before we were ready to leave. It was so cuddly and warm. He must have told his mother because a few weeks earlier I mentioned how I hated cold wind blowing around my neck. Sometimes it gives me headaches. Now I would be nice and warm.

Outside, with everyone heading home, Blanch tapped me on the shoulder. "Peggy, thank you for the doll. You couldn't have given me a better gift. I'm sorry for treating you so badly. Maybe you would like to come over and play dolls sometime."

I was so shocked I didn't know what to say. "Ok," was all I managed to squeak.

The following school day, cleaning up from the Christmas concert was our only task before getting report cards. By noon, everything was ship shape, setting us free until after New Year's. Students charged like cattle set free on a warm sunny day after being cooped up in the barn all winter. All we could talk about was skating, sliding and no schoolwork.

My most memorable day was the one before returning to school after the holidays. I was visiting Sally but didn't make it home before getting caught in a downpour. With warmer temperatures, snow turned to rain and I would have been soaked if it weren't for Blanch. She was walking toward me with an umbrella and without hesitating, came beside me, turned and held it so we both stayed dry. She walked me home. I thanked her wholeheartedly and upon reaching the door I urged, "Remember you suggested we play dolls? How about this afternoon?"

She agreed and we had a fabulous time together. Blanch actually turned out to be a nice person. "Can you keep a secret," she asked with a serious look.

"Sure I can, what is it?" My curiosity was overwhelming.

"Promise you won't tell anyone or hope to die?"

"Yes, I do."

"When you gave me the nice doll, I felt guilty even though I apologized. I want you to know, I don't like being mean, but I get angry when others won't play with me because my family is poor. I cover up by acting tough and mean, but it doesn't make me happy. You on the other hand are happy most of the time. I want to be like that. Do you think we could be friends?"

"Oh yes, friends are much nicer than enemies. Whenever we passed each other before, I didn't know what to say. Now it will be fun to bump into each other. Ha! Ha! Isn't that a silly expression? Before we got angry if we bumped into each other, now we'll be glad."

"Yes, you are right," Blanch agreed, as we laughed and pushed.

The golden rule really works. I was so happy to have another friend. Hopefully Sally would accept Blanch into our circle as well.

The next big event after Christmas was Valentine's Day. Creating cards with hearts, hugs and kisses took all afternoon at school. Miss Smith insisted everyone make one as she called it our art lesson. A few boys thought it was sissy stuff but didn't argue when they saw the look on Miss Smith's face. Charles and Richard took advantage of the opportunity, making cards so lovely the older girls hoped they would be the recipients. The boys just smiled while continuing their work. It was a mystery who got the cards, because nobody ever told.

Just before Easter I received a letter from Janet Fraser in Glen Margaret. We had met and hit it off wonderfully. She invited me to spend a few days with her during the holidays. I ran into the house to ask Mary. "Can I go, please, please?"

"Yes, Peggy, you may."

Glen Margaret School

"Thank you, Mary. This is going to be so much fun. She is having two other girls visit as well. We should have a grand time."

I could hardly wait for the day to arrive, but finally it did. The other nice thing was that Sally was going to

Big Tancook Island for a few days too. Now I wouldn't be lonely without her.

When I arrived, Joan and Emmy were already with Janet. I hadn't met them before but we all got along fine. We slept in the room above the kitchen. It was a cozy, large bedroom with the chimney inside, giving warmth, even becoming too hot at times. There was a large bed for two of us, and a spare mattress for the others. We got ready for bed early but talked into the wee hours in the night. We talked about school and the goings on. They had some wild stories to tell.

"Peggy, did you hear about Miss Hazel Herman," Janet asked.

"No. Why?"

"She taught in Glen Margaret for two years. Her home is down the south shore in a little place called Herman's Island, so she boards with the Redmond's. It seems all the teachers 'from away' stay there. The students feel sorry for Wayne, having a teacher live at his place and having her teach all day at school. I think he finds it a little much.

"Anyway, whenever she gets excited about something, which happens often, she talks so fast her false teeth fly out."

"Really Janet, that must look funny. Embarrassing too. What does she do when that happens?" I was very curious.

"Well, one day she was reading to a group of us. We were sitting in a circle near the potbelly stove. Miss Herman sneezed or something like that and her teeth went shooting across the floor. One little boy said she scooped them up so fast he didn't think they had stopped rolling before she had them back in her mouth. She didn't even wipe them off! Another time, they fell out when she was sitting at the desk and one of the students, Joyce Fraser, thought it was so funny seeing Miss Herman run around the desk and slap her teeth in her mouth quick as a wink. She must have had a lot of practice to be so quick and accurate. Seemed like it was all in one motion."

"You mean that actually happened," we all chorused.

"Oh yes, and there's more," Janet continued.

"She had her hands full with two students for sure, Blair and Jimmy. They got into fights often. One day, Blair was running from Jimmy and pulling desks in his path to slow him down. Jimmy was gaining so Blair charged out the door. Being determined to keep him out, Jimmy piled old unused desks against the door. The students thought this was great and watched and laughed. Poor Miss Herman was trying to keep order but stayed clear of Jimmy when he was mad. Meanwhile, Blair came around the side of the schoolhouse with big low windows. Jimmy couldn't see him as he was in the lobby. Jerry and Sam opened a window and pulled Blair inside. Well, that was quite a sight! Blair sat there watching Jimmy pile the desks sky high. Boy! Jimmy was furious when he discovered they made him look so foolish. There was terrible commotion until finally they both ran out of steam."

"My! My! My! That's terrible! Didn't the parents do anything about them being so bad? "

"Nobody knows. Miss Herman spoke to their parents but the fighting didn't stop."

Emmy and Joan sat wide-eyed as Janet told us more.

"Often Jimmy made us laugh by showing off. One of his favorite tricks was getting out of his seat so Miss Herman would try putting him back. As she took hold of him, he grabbed her in his arms like they were dancing. She got very upset and did her best to control him, but he was too strong and she was so little. Once he told the class he was going to kiss her. Sure enough he managed to give her a little peck on the cheek. It was pretty funny. She was trying to keep him away with one hand while hoping to get him seated with the other.

"Another time, Miss Herman finally forced Jimmy into his seat. Well, she had Jimmy pinned with her right hand holding the back of the desk and the left holding the front. Hard as he tried, Jimmy couldn't get out. Then his eyes lit up like a light and a big smile crossed his face.

"'Watch this everyone' he said.

"Now remember Miss Herman couldn't see his face but we could. He opened his mouth wide as he could and bit her arm. She let go instantly while giving a big yelp as Jimmy ran to freedom."

"Did you ever get any school work done?" I wondered.

"Surprisingly, some did. Others were too lazy. They failed," Janet replied.

"There's more believe it or not! One day, a few students were acting up just before school was out, so Miss Herman wouldn't let anyone go home. After a while she let the well-behaved students go. Teacher's pet's the bad kids called them. Alex and Sam growled and complained. Hoping to teach the boys patience and respect, she made sure they were the last ones there. Miss Herman was guarding the door so Alex suggested they go out the window. After all, she couldn't be in two places at once. To the window they went and crawled out. Sam, the youngest, was afraid but wanted to prove he wasn't a coward. Miss Herman saw them and threatened them enough so they both came back inside. She picked Sam to be taught a lesson, as he was smaller than Alex, who was a strong fellow. Sam told us she took him by the back of his shirt collar and twisted it almost choking him to death! Then she grabbed that thing kids dreaded most, the strap! Since Sam wouldn't hold out his hand, she gave him a number of belts wherever she could hit. Poor Sam lost all his bravery that day as he cried and yelled far more than necessary. He thought she would slack off if he made her think he was dying. That was the last time Sam went out the window."

"Your stories are funny, Janet. Do you have any more," asked Joan?

"Oh, I can tell a few more. Aren't you tired of hearing them?"

"No," Emmy insisted. "Go on."

"Okay, if you want me too. I saw this one from start to finish.

"On rainy days most children wear rubber boots. As you know, they are great for splashing through puddles and keeping your feet dry. One foggy, drizzly day, Sam wore his rubber boots. Somehow at recess, he and his brother Tom got into a fight. Well, Tom was bigger and stronger so had no problem holding him in a headlock.

"Oh! I must mention, Miss Herman wasn't the teacher when this happened. Miss Myra was, and boy was she strict! Nobody got out of their seats, talked without permission, or misbehaved.

"Sam was embarrassed, especially since he lost the fight in front of girls. Fighting wasn't allowed but the teacher was inside so they got away with it. After a few minutes Miss Myra rang the bell, ending recess. Tom had just let Sam go in time so they didn't get caught. We had to line up going into the school and Sam was right behind his brother. He was still fuming mad. Miss Myra always stood by the outer door, making sure all the kids came in. There was a lobby between the outer door and classroom. Just as they were going through the second doorway, Sam got ready to kick Tom in the seat of his pants. Well, he wound up his left leg with all his might and let go with every ounce of power he could muster up. There was a terrible bang as Sam's foot hit the doorjamb. He thought every bone and toe in his foot was broken as he hobbled to his desk. You know how a ruler vibrates when held on the edge of the desk and is snapped. That's how he described the feeling in his foot. Those rubber boots gave hardly any protection when his toes met the wood. Sam never tried that one again either. Sometimes it's a hard lesson. Later, Sam was glad he didn't kick his brother because he was sure he would have badly hurt him. He told that story in church to the children so they wouldn't fight or take revenge. After all he said, you might be the one getting hurt like I did.

"Are you girls sure you want to hear more," Janet asked, "I'm doing all the talking."

"Keep going, our turn will come, this is too funny," I coaxed.

"All right, this one involved Sam and his oldest brother, Louis. We play this game called 'Got-You-Last'. The idea is to tag a person and say, 'I got you last'. Nobody, and I mean nobody, liked being 'gotten last'. Miss Myra was writing on the board. The only two things students were permitted to do without asking was sharpen pencils and get a book from the library. Our library was no more than a bookcase with a large dictionary and reading books. Well, Louis sharpened his pencil and as he passed Sam, quickly touched him, whispering, 'I got you last' and hurried back to his seat. Now, Louis was separated from the others in the row by three desk spaces, just in front of the library. Sam was not happy, and decided to get Louis 'last' but his desk was in the very front of that row. While Miss Myra continued writing, Sam quietly sneaked to the back and with the tip of his foot touched Louis' outstretched foot. Glowing with delight, Sam headed for his seat hoping not to be caught by Miss Myra. Was he in for a surprise! Louis lifted his foot and hooked into Sam's. With Sam's momentum and Louis' solid position, both Sam's feet left the floor as he fell with a loud crash. There was no keeping his secret from Miss Myra now. That meant another day of staying after school, something Sam hated. The whole school wondered how he was going to get out of this one. Well, Sam's quick thinking saved the day. He quietly got up, went to the bookcase, took the dictionary and walked to his desk. Miss Myra watched in wonder but never said a word. That's the only time I ever saw Sam enjoy looking up words in the dictionary.

"Another time, one of the Westhaver boys wanted the afternoon off rather than go to school. He and a few boys broke branches off spruce trees, put them in the stove and closed the damper, causing smoke to fill the room. They did it during lunch when the teacher was home for dinner. It worked a few times but after that Mrs. Cooke, who was the teacher at that time, opened the windows and doors making the school air out enough for us to stay. Even the boys didn't like the smoky room so that put an end to those tricks.

"Trying to scare the teacher was always a favourite for all the boys. One time, Lee found a snake and put it in the drawer of the teacher's desk. She was mad and accused Mackenzie of doing it since he was laughing so hard. Not wanting to squeal on Lee, Mackenzie said nothing. He got a number of cracks on each hand with the strap.

"Another favourite of the boys was locking the toilet door while we were inside. They always did it just before the bell rang. After noticing a few vacant seats, the teacher wondered where we were. Of course, the boys acted so innocent it would make you sick. Someone said they heard noise at the back of the school. Betty was sent outside to see what happened, heard us banging on the door and let us out.

"The boys put tacks on our seats, too. You must always look carefully before sitting, especially when returning to your desk. All those who saw the tack being put on the seat couldn't wait for the yell and jump of the girl. It was no funny matter if you were one. I know! Only once did I forget to check and plopped onto my seat. I can tell you one thing; I got up a lot faster than I sat down. Pulling it out hurt!

"Anyway, I'm getting tired of talking," Janet yawned. "Someone else tell us what goes on in your school. How about you, Joan."

"We had some pretty funny things happen too. I don't know if you'll like them as much as Janet's, but here goes anyway.

"At our school in Seabright, David Boutilier, that's Uncle Willie's nephew, had a bad habit of whispering. The teacher couldn't get him to stop. After telling him over and over, she finally said, "Enough is enough, David, you come here." Then she made him sit under the desk where her feet would be. He must have been bored. Later he told us he remembered the jackknife in his pocket. He quietly whittled a hole just big enough to get his tongue through. Sticking his tongue through the hole caught our eye. We couldn't stop laughing as he kept sticking it out. Of course, the more we laughed, the more he did it. Poor Mrs. Hubley couldn't figure out what was going on and no way were we going to tell her! We were having too much fun. It was a long time before she found his secret of getting the class laughing so hard."

"That's a good one Joan, tell us more," I begged.

"Okay! Sue had a problem with being talkative too. After being warned, the teacher finally put her out in the lobby. That's the little room at the entrance of the school where wood or coal is stored. Not wanting to be stuck there, Sue decided she had enough of this and ran all the way home to the end of Umlah's Road, over a mile. She told her mother what happened. Well, her mother sent her right back. Sue knew she would be in real big trouble if the teacher found out. So she ran all the way back hoping nobody would know what she did. Once in the lobby, she quietly hid behind the woodpile, out of sight. Only minutes later, the teacher came out and not seeing her called her name.

"Sue said, 'yes', and looked up over the woodpile.

"'Oh! There you are.'

"While going into the class, Mrs. Hubley said, 'See, she was there behind the woodpile all along.' Obviously the teacher had sent a student out to check on Sue and couldn't find her. Sue had a sheepish smile as she came into the class and later told us how happy she was not to have been caught.

"From what Sue told me, she had a history of getting into trouble. Even in grade one she made the teacher mad. Having free time, she asked if she could draw on the board and the teacher said yes. Sue drew a chicken, then a nest and finally the hen laying three eggs. Everyone laughed and when Mrs. Hubley saw the drawing, she told Sue to erase it immediately. Sue was puzzled but later found out that everyone thought the chicken was laying droppings instead of eggs."

"You all have such funny stories. We didn't have those things happening at our school," I said.

"Emmy, you tell them about the boys smoking," insisted Joan.

Emmy began, "One of Sue's older brothers, along with three or four other teenage boys, smoked during the lunch hour on their way back to school. Mrs. Hubley made them hold out their hands so she could smell them. Every time she got a whiff of cigarette smoke, they got the strap. Knowing they would be caught again, they looked for a way out. They found either horse manure or a cow patty and decided to rub it over their hands. Sure enough, Mrs. Hubley did the smelling test. Was she wild when she took a deep breath! The stink told her she had been tricked but she couldn't prove they were smoking. They didn't get the strap that day because the smell of manure covered the cigarette smoke.

"I have one more story," Emmy said.

"Sue and the kids from Umlah's Road fought with the kids from Redmond's Road. They threw rocks at each other just about every day hoping to get the others on the run. A parent asked Mrs. Hubley to keep the Umlah Road kids in school a few minutes later so the Redmond's Road kids could get a head start. The teacher agreed but the problem wasn't solved because they were waiting for them and started the whole thing over again. Finally, Sue told the teacher it was useless keeping them late since the others weren't going home but waiting for them by their turnoff. Sue convinced the teacher and they weren't kept late again. It was a miracle nobody got hurt by all those flying rocks."

By the time we finished our stories, all four of us were yawning and settling off to sleep. What a time we had though! Now I could tell all my friends at the Cove what went on in other schools.

Before long, school would be over for another year. Everyone was excited. I had mixed feelings. The freedom all summer pleased me but not what was to come with it. James would be finished grade nine. There was talk about what he would do. He loved sailing and had a chance to work on the schooner owned by Captain Simms who lived in Seabright, about midway in St. Margaret's Bay. Captain Simms shipped fish and supplies to parts of the Maritimes. Sometimes they were gone for a long, long time, up to month or two if he went to Newfoundland or Labrador. That meant James would be away a lot. I had grown fond of him because he understood my feelings and was always looking out for me. I hoped he would change his mind and go fishing with John or someone else. Time would tell.

Christmas Season

As Christmas approached, villagers prepared for the festive days ahead. A major family outing was the cutting of the Christmas tree. With axe in hand, we ventured through the barrens deep into the woods where fir trees grew plentiful.

"This is so peaceful, listening to the squeaking of fresh snow under our boots," I said to everyone.

"Yes it certainly is," Mary agreed. "And the scenery is breathtaking. Coming here each year is always a wonderful experience; absorbing this beautiful creation. These snow-covered landscapes are a paradise for artists."

"Yes, there's no doubt about that," agreed John.

"You are both right," I said. "But my legs are wanting to rest. How much farther?"

"Not far now, Peggy," John assured me. "Too bad we weren't on the Dover Road toward the far end."

"Why is that," I wanted to know.

John chuckled, "Because there is a rock nestled under a large tree beside the road known as the Sofa Rock. It's shaped like a sofa, giving weary travelers like you a comfortable resting place."

"Oh! Yes! That's just what I need," I gasped.

We all laughed.

He was right. After a couple of turns in the path, we came to a large clearing where a great number of young fir trees peppered the hills.

"How did so many trees get here," I asked.

"Some years ago, loggers cleared the area allowing new growth to thrive," John explained.

All three boys along with John, Mary and myself, searched for the perfect tree. We found four nice shaped trees, and after carefully looking over each one, we made our choice. Mary thought Joe's was the best. We all agreed.

James cut it down, and he and John carried our prize tree so it wouldn't get damaged. Every family tried to get the best tree possible and we were sure this year ours would be the envy of the community. Of course, all trees look great when decorated.

Excitement grew each day, especially after the tree was decorated. Everyone took part in placing ornaments in their favourite spots. By Christmas Eve I was so excited, I could hardly sleep through the night. Oh, how slowly the hours dragged by. I did manage to get a little shuteye but woke up from the sounds John was making downstairs as he added wood to the fire. He had already finished the morning barn chores as a treat for the boys.

Whispers from Joe, Peter and James reached my straining ears. They were getting up. I wasn't going to miss out, so dressing quickly, I crept downstairs with them. John met us at the bottom of the stairs with a smile while saying, "Merry Christmas. You didn't think you could sneak down here without me knowing, did you?"

"Well, we tried," James said, with a big grin.

"Now remember, there is no peeking into the gifts but you can open one present from your stocking."

"Look at all the gifts." I was overwhelmed.

Under the tree were stacks of nicely wrapped packages. Neatly arranged on the mantle were four stockings, stuffed with goodies and small packages beckoning our call. I wanted to rip them open right away.

Shaking and feeling gifts kept us guessing until Mary came downstairs to prepare breakfast. Their tradition was to have breakfast before opening presents. Waiting was hard and took forever.

After eating breakfast and washing dishes, Mary said we could open our gifts.

"Oh, goody," I said. "It's been a long wait!"

"Yes, I know Peggy, I remember when I was your age too. It's the same with all kids. You will change when you get older."

"I don't think so", I assured her.

We took turns so everyone could see the surprised look on our faces and what we had. It made the gift time last longer too.

James was thrilled with his very own compass, Peter felt like a man with his hunting knife, and Joe and I were overwhelmed with new skates. Although I didn't know how to skate, I was determined to learn and longed to glide over the ice like other kids. Mary made nice warm socks, mittens and a wooly warm sweater for each of us. She must have worked hard during school time and nights when we were asleep to do all that. A game of Chinese checkers was a family gift.

We ran errands and did odd jobs for our neighbours to earn money to purchase gifts for Mary and John. For Mary, James helped us make new circular heat pads from rope. There were three large and three small ones. Her favourite gift was the pair of leather gloves we had bought for her.

"Oh! My! You children are wonderful. That's

exactly the kind I wanted and how nice to have brand new heating pads to protect the table. Thank you very much."

For John, we bought a new drawknife. His old one had a broken handle. He used it a lot, especially in the spring for peeling bark off trees. Sap releases bark from a tree just like grease releases bread from a pan.

"Thank you all. How'd you know that was what I wanted?"

"Oh! A little birdie told us," we chorused while laughing.

"Yes, I'm sure she did, and I think I know her name."

It was such a happy time with everyone sharing.

John helped us clean up the wrapping paper while Mary headed toward the kitchen to prepare Christmas dinner. She was blessed with a talent for making food taste so good. There were a few vegetables we didn't take kindly to, one being turnip. Mary was determined we have a portion of whatever was prepared. That was the rule. Nobody made a fuss but we gulped those kinds of vegetables quickly so the remaining meal could be enjoyed. As time passed, John must have found better seeds for those detestable vegetables since we got to like nearly all of them. There was one culprit that required years before adjusting to our taste buds, even with a dousing of vinegar or lemon juice. Spinach! I still remember how slimy it felt in my mouth. Our poor stomachs worked hard digesting, since we chewed very little before swallowing it. Mary insisted greens were important so even our rolling eyes didn't stop her from serving it.

James suggested we play our new game of checkers.

"What a good idea," Joe said.

Since I didn't know how to play the game very well

and James was a master, we challenged Peter and Joe. It was a most exciting time since both teams won and lost. I was the cause for our losses but James, being such a great sport, made me feel losing was a good experience.

"It helps build character," he said.

Later John came over and said, "Can I play?"

"Sure Dad," they said with a smile, knowing very well whoever played against him was sure to lose. He was unbeatable to all family members. Sure enough, as the boys took turns one by one, he beat them but James gave him a run for his money. Then they made me play against him. Surprise! I won.

John laughed as he said, "Great game Peggy, you are an excellent player. It's been a long time since anyone beat me."

I was so excited I ran bubbling to Mary, "Mary, I won, I won."

"Yes, I heard, I can see you are overjoyed."

Of course I knew he let me win but it was fun anyway and a valuable lesson I hoped I would never forget.

John said, "It was worth losing just seeing you jump for joy. We knew you would be happy but not that much."

I learned making others happy was more important than winning, especially if it's only a game.

James advised, "Remember, give the underdog a break, you'll be glad you did."

Voices outside and a knock on the door distracted our attention from checkers to curiosity as to who was there.

"Come out and slide with us," encouraged a group of kids, anxious to break in their new sleds. "There's enough snow for sliding so come and join us."

Mary said, "Go ahead, you have time as dinner will be a little later than usual. You have over two hours."

Dressing quickly, we headed to the shed for our sleighs. They were hanging in a row on the wall held by pegs. James handed them to us. He hesitated when picking up Elizabeth's, now to be mine. It must have brought back memories because his eyes blinked quickly a few times as he gently placed it in my hands.

Everyone was quiet for a second when Peter broke the silence by saying, "Come on, they're waiting for us."

As everyone lined up to race down the slope, Billy warned us not to run and jump on the sled until the snow was packed. A friend of his, Leslie, broke his front tooth when the runners hit the ground and stopped short. That caused his head to go forward, hitting his tooth on the front of the sled. It was the first snow and his first ride of the year. Billy's advice was heeded, and there were no accidents to spoil our special day.

I couldn't count the number of times we went up and down the hill that day, but my growling stomach told me dinnertime must be close. Minutes later, Mary rang the big cowbell. That was a signal dinner was almost ready. She copied the idea from Mrs. Fraser in Glen Margaret. Mrs. Fraser had a giant cowbell and rang it to let her husband know dinner would be ready by the time he got home. He didn't have a pocket watch but could hear the bell while gardening, making hay or even back over the hill where he cut wood.

An appetizing aroma of baked chicken and apple pie made our mouths water. Yummy! The smell caused my taste buds to tingle just thinking about the good food. I blocked the thought of turnip and such out of my mind.

John and Mary invited a neighbour, Mr. Garrison, to join us. He was alone after his wife passed away and had no family to spend Christmas with. He complimented Mary by saying, "Mary that was a fine meal. Cooking isn't something I do very well. Thanks to considerate folks like you, I don't have to prepare most of my own meals. I get a lot of invitations and sometimes meals brought to my home. I appreciate your kindness."

Everyone helped put away food and wash dishes except Mr. Garrison and John. They relaxed and chatted. With four eager kids to go outside, everything was finished in no time. That gave us the opportunity to play the rest of the afternoon.

The bigger boys cleared a large area on the nearby lake for skating. I could only imagine what the experience would be like. Well, was I in for a surprise, just standing on skates took skill. After a number of falls, and much determination, I managed to move somewhat. A few small children and I were the only beginners. Others whizzed by showing off their fancy skating skills. Fortunately, Sally arrived about mid-afternoon, instructing me how to move legs, body, and arms. She made it look so simple and I improved quickly with her coaching.

As daylight lessened, we knew it was time to head home. Milder winds brought warm air, making the snow sticky. We were all taking off our skates when Sally threw a snowball at Peter. He ducked allowing a clear path for a direct hit on the back of James' neck.

"Ahhh!" he yelled. "Who threw that?"

Blanch pointed to Sally who stood there with a hand over her mouth in disbelief.

"I didn't mean to James. I was aiming for Peter."

"Sure you were," James yelled while laughing and throwing a handful of snow at her.

Others joined in the fun and, in moments, snow was flying everywhere. When Blanch wasn't looking, Sally got her good. Of course, with snowballs going in every direction, it was unlikely anyone knew who threw what. It was all in good fun. A couple of the older boys threw girls into a snow bank. I wasn't positive but it sure looked like Stephen tried kissing Ruby, although he made it look like an accident. "Isn't that silly," I thought. When everyone was worn out, peace reigned, allowing time to gather our belongings and head for home. Some bragged about how they got this or that person with a snowball.

"Payday is coming and we'll get you when you're least expecting it," the snowball victims promised.

We all agreed it was a glorious day.

"Don't you wish Christmas was every day," I said. They all laughed, but said it was a good idea.

There was just enough daylight to quickly do our chores before supper. Mary insisted Mr. Garrison stay for the evening meal as well. He didn't want to intrude but never argued when John told him he better listen to Mary.

"You don't want to ruffle her feathers, do you?"

"Oh, no siree I don't," was his reply but his smile told he was happy for the invitation.

"You people are so kind," he said. "It's wonderful to have such good neighbours."

John replied, "Christmas is a time for sharing, not just getting gifts."

Mary reinforced John's statement by saying, "That's right, always share and you will be blessed."

After eating, we listened to fascinating stories of good and bad times throughout Mr. Garrison's life. My only problem was I couldn't stay awake. Playing in the fresh air had worn me out. My eyelids were heavy and the pillow wouldn't be reached soon enough to bring sweet rest. Mary tucked me in and kissed me good night. I'm sure dreamland arrived before she reached the door.

Pranks and Unusual Happenings

Only a few weeks with my new family had passed when Halloween arrived. Every young person in the Cove was talking about who they were going to dress up as. They wanted to know what my plans were but I hadn't decided yet.

When I got home, I asked Mary if she had any idea what I should do. "Yes", she said, "I have a surprise for you. For the last few days, I have been sewing a costume and it's almost finished. Why don't you see how it fits?" She brought out a beautiful angel outfit. With a few minor adjustments, it fit perfectly.

"Oh Mary, you are too much," I said as I gave her a big hug.

"I'm glad you like it. I have a mask too so folks won't know who you are."

I was so excited I couldn't wait to tell Sally, since we planned to go trick-or-treating together. As for the boys, James said he was too old for that nonsense but was going to a party at a friend's house. Peter planned to be an Indian and Joe decided he was dressing as a pirate with a wooden leg and a patch on one eye. Rain was falling but, with one day left, we hoped the weather would change.

Sure enough, by noon the next day, sunshine broke through the clouds now and then. By evening, fog rolled in but there was no rain. The fog gave the night a creepy feeling but I felt safe knowing I would be with Sally.

We worked at our chores right after school so we could have supper and be ready to go by dark. Mary invited Sally for supper so we could leave together.

Sally's costume was a witch's outfit so we looked very different. Her mother has artistic talents that gave her the ability to create a *papier maché* mask that looked almost like a real person. We were sure nobody would guess who we were. By the time we were ready, dusk had fallen so off we went. That night was so much fun. Most people couldn't guess who we were and some wouldn't give any treats unless we took our masks off. There wasn't one home we didn't visit. Our pillowcases grew heavy with cookies, apples, popcorn balls, candy and other goodies.

The last house we stopped at had a party going on. James was inside and not looking too happy. I later learned his date took an interest in someone else. I asked if he would come with Sally and me. He agreed. I think he wanted an excuse to leave anyway. Now, I wouldn't have to walk from her house to ours all by myself.

About half way to our place, just where it was darkest, we heard strange 'whoooo whoooo' sounds. As we looked in the direction of the noise, three white figures slowly moved back and forth. My heart raced as I thought of ghosts chasing us. I grabbed James' arm while holding on for dear life. "What is it?" I whispered.

"Oh, it's probably some boys trying to scare us", James said in a low voice. "You just watch this." He removed his arm from my grasp and raced straight for them. Well, you should have seen what happened. Those three figures ran like the dickens. James caught one and pulled off the sheet to reveal one of the Morash boys.

"Hold it James, it's only me, Steven," he yelled. The other two returned, took off the sheets and had a great laugh. It was Michael and Vincent. They told how some ran like crazy when they saw three ghosts.

"How come you weren't scared James?"

"Because I don't believe in ghosts. Being Halloween, I just figured some guys were out to have some fun, so I decided to have a little myself."

"Yeah, you were the first one to come after us," they explained. After chatting a few minutes, we parted and said good night.

I held James' hand all the way home. That was too scary for me. "Oh James, you are so brave, I would have died if you weren't with me," I said. He gave a big laugh but I could tell he had a grin on his face and seemed to be walking a bit taller.

As we entered the house, I excitedly told John and Mary how James rescued me from three ghosts. "Oh really," they said. Then we explained who they were. I emptied my sack of goodies with a smile that told I was well pleased.

Right at that moment, Peter and Joe burst through the door. "We just saw three ghosts," they shouted.

"No," said James, "really?"

"Yes, we did, and they even chased us. It's a good thing we could run faster because they nearly caught us." They could hardly talk as they were so out of breath. All four of us burst out laughing while Peter and Joe stood there looking bewildered. "We did see them," they protested.

"Yes," said James. "So did Peggy and I."

"You did!" Joe said in shock.

Then I told them how James was my hero and saved me. They just stood there shaking their heads.

"Don't you tell anyone about this," they threatened.

"Don't worry, the whole village will know tomorrow when the Morash boys tell of their adventures," said James.

"Boys oh boys, are we going to be laughed at," said Peter.

"Oh don't take it too seriously, there are plenty of others they sacred too," James assured. But they still weren't happy with being thought of as scaredy cats.

Mary brought us back to reality when she told us it was time to get ready for bed. "Remember, there is school you know."

"Oh yeah," we all moaned. We were having such a nice time together I didn't want it to stop. As I settled down, I did notice the sandman was knocking at my door. It still took a while for sleep to come as I thought about the fun that I had that night, especially being saved by my second hero, James.

Before school closed for the summer, I spent a few days with Janet again. All the community teachers were meeting with the school board representatives so Monday was a holiday. That gave me the weekend with Janet. Somehow we got talking about tricks and pranks which led to the subject of Halloween. Traditionally, Halloween was the time boys played tricks on their neighbours. Not only at Peggy's Cove but also in every community throughout the Bay. Pranks were the delight of young people, so whenever opportunity knocked, they were sure to take advantage of the situation.

"Those boys did an awful thing to Willie Covey," Janet confided.

"Like what," I wanted to know.

"Willie, from Hackett's Cove, owned a wagon that had small wheels at the front and big wheels on the back. Last Halloween, a group of boys got together and switched the wheels so the big ones were on the front and little ones on back. Next morning, Willie hitched up his wagon with the oxen and couldn't figure what was wrong. He knew something was odd but just couldn't put his finger on it. Finally he headed to Bob Pace's at the Three Brooks hoping he could see the problem. It didn't take Bob long before he chuckled and told Willie what happened the night before. Poor Willie felt so stupid. We often wondered why he couldn't figure it out."

It was normal every Halloween to upset toilets, and either place gates on a barn roof, hide them or even switch with a neighbour's if there was any way to make it fit. The school toilets seemed to be a particular favourite target, in hopes of a day off perhaps. Some schools had doubles where the boys and girls used one building with a wall between. It must have taken a number of boys to tip those over. The community men would come to raise them and sometimes required the strength of oxen or a horse. It was all very amusing to the kids of the community to see what was done through the night.

"Did anyone ever get hurt doing all those tricks," I asked.

"Not that I know of but this one wasn't good for the cow I can tell you," Janet replied.

"A cow," I said, "Tell me what they did to it."

"This was a terrible Halloween trick. Percy owned a brown cow but when he looked out the next morning, a white one was in his pasture instead. He was puzzled because nobody had a white cow in Indian Harbour and he could see the fence wasn't broken or the gate left open. It looked like his cow by the shape but not the colour. He figured he better get a closer look. Boy, was he surprised when he saw someone had whitewashed poor Bessy through the night. Fortunately, whitewash comes off with water. After giving her a good bath, she was back to her normal colour."

"That was mean, those boys should have been punished," I said.

"They couldn't be. No one ever said who did it."

Just then we heard a voice.

"Janet would you and Peggy deliver this package to Beatrice for me please?" called Mrs. Fraser. "If you do, I'll let you buy some candy at Maher's store and you can have it for a treat after dinner."

"Oh yes, Mother, we would like that, wouldn't we Peggy? But do we have to wait until after dinner to eat it? Can't we have it on our way home?" Janet pleaded.

"Now you know better than to even ask, don't you? Eating candy before dinner will spoil you appetite."

"Oh, all right."

"Dinner should be ready by the time you get back. That is if you don't dilly dally."

As we started out, I asked, "Who is Beatrice?"

"Beatrice and George are brother and sister who live just up the road a bit, neither having married. They have some strange ways, which we think are funny. Often boys throw rocks at George's bark pot. It's down by the road, close to his fish store. You'll see it. When he hears the banging or sees them throwing rocks he runs down the hill in hopes of catching them. But they take off before he can get near. One day he was in the toilet and charged out pulling up his overalls, fastening them as he chased after the boys. I often wondered what he would do if he managed to catch one of them.

"Beatrice is a kind, happy lady and always has a smile for everyone. She earns money by sewing for those who are unable to or prefer her fine work instead of their own. George isn't quite as cheerful or as industrious as

George's House and Bark Pot

Beatrice. He does the yard and house maintenance, milks the cow, feeds the chickens and plants the garden. He is fortunate enough to own a berth, which brings income without working. His berth is behind Little Thrum (known to us as Little Trumpcap), which is a good place to set a trap. He rents it to Gerald and Garnet Fralick. When Gerald goes to pay George, they always go to the front room so Beatrice won't know how much money George gets. They are really nice people, they just have some strange ways."

"Like what?" I asked.

"No doubt they'll be cooking dinner. You look at the pots on the stove and see if you notice anything different or strange. If you don't, I'll tell you on our way back."

"Oh, Peggy, see that boat hauled up on the launch over there."

"Yes, what about it?"

"That belongs to the Harnish's. And see that barrel of molasses at the side of Charlie Maher's store? He leaves it outside in a large keg since nobody steals any; there isn't even a lock on the spout. One evening, Mr. Harnish came back from fishing and forgot to take his rubber boots with him. They were still in the boat. A couple of fellows saw them, went over to the molasses barrel and put about a cup of molasses in each boot. The next day when Mr. Harnish put them on, he was disgusted with the gooey feeling inside. Even more so when he learned someone played a trick on him."

"Mac lives in that house, the one before George's. I have a story about him too."

"Let me hear it," I said.

"Sometimes folks don't put their horses or oxen into the barn or pasture at night. They just let them roam and feed wherever they can find hay. One night

Mackenzie was coming home in the pitch dark. He didn't bother with a lantern because he knew the road so well getting home was usually no problem. All of a sudden he ran into something big and black. A huge animal made weird noises and Mac ran for home as fast as he could. Later he learned it was someone's black horse standing sideways in the middle of the road. Mac said he didn't know who was scared the most, him or the horse."

"This is Beatrice's road. That's their house on top of the hill. The back door is the one they use so we'll go in there instead of the front one," Janet explained.

"Hello Janet, who is your friend?" asked George, who was heading inside with an armload of wood as we rounded the corner of the house.

"This is Peggy. She is visiting me."

"Y-You wouldn't be P-P-Peggy of the Cove by any chance?" he stuttered.

"Well yes, that's what some people call me," I shyly responded.

"Well! Well! Well! Come on in, B-Beatrice, this is the famous little P- Peggy of the C-Cove," he said. "Isn't she a pr-pr-pretty little thing?"

"Yes, she is George. Peggy, I'm so pleased to meet you, we've heard so much about you. I'm glad Janet is your friend." I noticed she was sitting in a wheel chair while tending food on the stove.

"Thank you, I'm pleased to meet you too. Everyone is so nice to me. And yes, Janet is my special friend."

I couldn't help noticing the string hanging out over the top of one pot. Was that what Janet meant? I wondered. Curious, I asked, "I have never seen string coming out of a pot before, what's it for?"

"Oh that's on George's piece of meat. That way he can keep his separate from mine but we save from dirtying more dishes by cooking it in the same pot," Beatrice replied.

"Y-Yes and ah! If I'm not c-c-careful she'll eat my vegetables too," George responded. "That's w-why I cut mine in a different s-s-shape than hers. See," he said, as he lifted the lid on the other two pots.

Sure enough, the potatoes were almost divided in half but on the left all were small and round. On the right, they were cut in two or three pieces but definitely easy to tell apart. The carrots were cut in round pieces and others in long strips.

"D-Don't you t-t-think that's a good idea?" George asked. "That way B- Beatrice can't eat my dinner."

I smiled but wanted to burst out laughing, Now I knew what Janet meant when she said they had strange ways. Lucky for me a kitten rubbed against my leg while meowing for food or attention.

"What a pretty cat," I said, while bending down to scratch its ears and to hide my smile, which almost turned into laughter."

"That's Daisy," replied Beatrice. "She is the best mouser you could ever want. We have more cats but they don't catch mice like Daisy."

"Here's the package from Mother," Janet said. "We better get back. Dinner will soon be ready."

"Have a cookie," Beatrice insisted.

"Mother told us not to eat before dinner," Janet replied.

"Oh yes, but just this once won't matter. Besides, I won't tell if you don't. Isn't that right, George?" Beatrice warned.

"Y-Yes, B-Beatrice, whatever you s-say."

"Thank you" we said, while biting into one. "Oh yes, these are good. Yummy!" and started for the door.

Heading down the hill, we both burst out laughing.

"Now I know what you meant about having strange ways. That is so funny. They are nice people though," I said.

"Let's run to see how fast we can go down this steep part of the hill," Janet suggested.

Off we went. It was hard to keep our feet in balance with our bodies; the hill was so steep. Just at the bottom I noticed a cow flop at the last second. I tried to jump over it.

"Oh, no! Yuk, my heel hit the cow flop," I said to Janet.

"Phew," Janet said, "too bad it's a fresh one. Let's clean off your shoe in the grass over here. You're lucky your foot didn't go in the center of it. Just think of the mess that would have made."

"You're absolutely right, Janet. That would have been a disaster."

We cleaned my shoe and hurried into the store for the candy.

"Janet, do you have any more stories. I think they are funny."

"Yes, I know another one."

"Tell me"

"Everyone has a jug for molasses that the storekeeper will fill. You know from the barrel I pointed out earlier. After its full he puts a cork on top. One night, Ross was sent to the store to get the jug filled. Unfortunately, the store was out of molasses so Ross was out of luck. A group of men were sitting around telling ghost stories. Ross couldn't help but hear them and then headed home alone. At first, he was not afraid but all of a sudden the wind blew quite hard. He heard a 'whoooooo ooooohhh' sound. He thought for sure a ghost was after him and lost all sense of reason. He ran home so fast, that when he got there the family thought he was going to die from exhaustion. He was so out of breath. After telling them about being chased by a ghost, his father figured out what happened. The wind blew across the opening of the jug, making a noise that sounded like a ghost. His folks had a great laugh but Ross didn't think it so funny."

By the time we finished story telling, we arrived home right on time for dinner.

"Did everything go all right?" Mrs. Fraser asked.

"Yes, just fine," replied Janet, without saying anything about the cookie. "Peggy saw how they cook their food so it keeps separate. We think that's so odd."

"Well, it's not nice to make fun of people but it is a bit humorous I must admit," said Mrs. Fraser.

After dinner, we played and ran up the hill to get another look at the Bay. The watering hole had a lot of frogs, and we wanted to catch some. It took a long time because they were so quick. We sat on top of the big rock enjoying the warmth while chatting. We saw John coming, and we hurried down the hill so he wouldn't have to wait for me.

Fraser's Hill

Just as we were going past the Wolf River apple tree, Janet yelled, "Look out! Skunk!"

We both stopped in our tracks and ran away just in time.

"Oh, thank you Janet. That would have been a

disaster. I shiver just thinking about it. What a horrible ending that would have been to a perfect weekend." I gathered my things and we headed for home. I talked John's ears off the whole trip telling him about all the fun we had.

The early days of summer brought sweet songs of cheerful birds, fresh smells from blooming flowers and the smell of newly mowed hay drying in the field. Haymaking was something I couldn't remember doing before, it was a new experience for me. It was a happy time but not for all. Some kids would rather be swimming, fishing or doing another favourite pastime rather than work. For me, I enjoyed shaking, turning and stacking hay but especially the hay wagon ride. On a perfect day, John rose early and mowed with the scythe while we shook hay for drying. In the early afternoon, it was turned to dry on the other side, hopefully, by suppertime. We raked the hay in neat windrows, ready to be loaded onto the wagon and taken to the barn before dark. That didn't happen often because few days were ideal. Most times it took two days with sunshine to have perfect hay, sometimes longer.

Occasionally, rain threatened the drying process, often halfway through, so we made haystacks and covered them with a tarp. The plus side was they made great hiding places when playing hide and seek, or a game of tag. Sometimes, we even hid inside a haystack by getting someone to lift the middle while we crawled inside. The idea was for the person who was "it" to give up because there was no way the kid who was hiding could see if it was safe to run to home base. The only problem being, if it was a long search, the heat became unbearable. We came out all hot and sweaty but it was worth the wait if we won.

We girls soon learned how to get the boys out in a hurry. One evening I couldn't find two fellows so I asked Sally, "Give me that pitchfork so I can stick it in the hay, I'll find out if anyone is in there." As Sally handed me the fork, I said, "Let's start with this one, I'll give it a good jab."

A cry of, "No Peggy, are you crazy, don't jab me with that fork," bellowed Stephen and echoed by Michael in the stack beside him. I ran quickly to base and got them out. The girls jumped and laughed with delight, as the boys raced for home base but not in time. A new rule was quickly put in place as the boys protested loudly. The rule stated, no pitchforks allowed! It wasn't the smartest thing to do. Someone could really get hurt badly or even blinded if hit in the eye. I wasn't really going to jab the pitchfork, I just wanted to scare them and make them come out. They didn't like being outsmarted by girls.

The mischievous boys weren't totally innocent. They got their jollies by chasing us girls whenever they found a snake. The more we screamed and ran, the longer the torture, unless an adult stopped them. Haymaking season annoyed snakes hiding amongst tall grass, making lots of chances for boys to terrify us.

Sally and I decided the boys were having too much fun scaring the daylights out of us. Action must be taken. We rounded up a few more girls and put our minds to serious thinking.

"What can we do to scare the boys?" Sally questioned. "We are tired of them getting the best of us." We all agreed.

Ruby said, "I wish a great, big giant snake would come out of a hole and scare them. Then they would know how we feel."

"That's it!" I cried.

"That's what, Peggy, tell us!"

"Well, you know how good Mary is at sewing. Let's get her to help us make a giant snake from cloth. She is very good at decorating too. She has light brown fabric and we could have her paint strips and spots like a huge garter snake. You know, like those big brown ones often sunning themselves on that little hill along the blueberry path. But this one will be really big and fat.'

"Oh, Peggy, that's a super idea but how are we going to scare the boys with it."

"I have an idea, let me tell you as we go ask Mary." So off we rushed, coaxing Mary to help.

Mary thought we were a little ambitious and maybe getting carried away but knew how we detested being chased. "Oh, all right, I'll do it. But you girls know the boys will retaliate," Mary warned.

"Yeah, but we don't care. It's time we taught them a lesson," Sally blurted.

"I'll need your help with peeling vegetables for supper and running to the store if I make it now."

"We'll do it," we all agreed. So each took up their assigned task with great excitement, thinking of the frightened looks on so-called brave boys.

After preparing the vegetables, the girls headed for the store. That's when I revealed the remainder of my plan.

"What a splendid idea," they agreed. "We will do it after supper when the boys gather to decide what excitement they will do tonight."

Mary made the snake look so real it was scary just looking at the thing. We knew it wasn't alive but it gave us shivers down our backs anyway.

Peggy ate quickly and asked to be excused. Mary, knowing the plan, let her go. Sally was waiting down by the wharf with a basket. Joe had caught a huge eel a few days before and was keeping it in a crate tied to the wharf. They carefully opened the top, caught it with a dip net and placed it in the basket. "Yuk, that is one big slimy eel," Sally said. "Do you think this is right?"

"I feel a little guilty too," I replied, "but we'll just borrow it for a while. You know eels live for hours out of water. When we finish, we'll put it back."

I had asked Mary to leave a hole midway in the belly of the snake on the bottom. That way we could push a stick inside without being noticed and make it lunge at the boys. Not until going to the store did Sally say she wished she knew how to make it wiggle like a live snake. That's when I thought of the eel. Now we really got excited. We decided to put the eel where the stick was supposed to be.

Carefully poking a fork handle through the hole, we made a tunnel big enough for the eel. We poured a little water on the bottom to keep it moist. Then, with great difficulty we managed to get the slimy thing in the hole. With its head inside, it squirmed into the tunnel with ease trying to escape. It was so real, Ruby, who arrived just after we slid the eel in, screamed when she saw it wiggling toward her.

"Ruby, be quiet, we'll get caught," we whispered.

"That thing gives me the willies. Are you sure it isn't alive?"

"Yes, it's the eel, remember."

Moving as not to cause attention, the girls got everything set. "Ok, Peggy, we're ready if you are."

"Yes, let's go."

Ruby and Sally told a number of girls of their plan to scare the boys and not to tell anyone. A dozen, or more, girls arrived at the back door of the barn, and climbed up into the haymow ready to watch the fun. They were warned not to scream when they saw the big snake.

The boys noticed a number of girls going to John's barn and began questioning what they were up to. Sally and Ruby went past them as they pretended to get something from Ruby's house, then came out a minute later. As they returned, the boys teased them about the snake chase earlier that day, calling them 'scaredy' cats. "Oh you guys just think you're something, don't you," snapped Sally. They laughed as boys do.

From a safe distance, Ruby and Sally yelled, "If you guys can catch us before we get to John's barn, we'll let you put a snake down our backs." The girls took off running but the boys ran after them as if being chased by a lion.

The girls ran past where I was, buried in a pile of hay with just a small opening to see through. I held the snake with one hand. It, too, was covered by hay with just the head sticking out. At the perfect moment, I squeezed the tail of the eel and gave the snake a big push. The boys came to a screeching stop as the snake charged towards them.

"Yikes! Look out, look out," one of them yelled.

You should have seen the look on their faces. Now where was their bravery! They made some weird noises while taking off in the opposite direction. Then Sally ran out, grabbed the snake by the neck and chased the boys a short distance. They couldn't believe this was happening. Quickly she returned to the barn, closed the big door, and slipped the eel into the basket. Then we hid the snake. The laughter was uncontrollable. We never laughed so hard in our lives. Oh, how happy we were to see those terrified boys. This was a day they would never forget.

"Did you see the look on their faces," Sally asked.

"Oh my, yes" said Ruby. "That was worth a thousand dollars."

"Let's get the eel back before they find out our secret," I whispered anxiously. "Ruby, you help me and we'll go out the back door."

We walked nonchalantly to the wharf, pulled the crate in, opened the top and tipped the basket to dump the eel back. But oh! Horrors of horrors! Squirming and wiggling, the front half of the eel hung over the outside and it quickly dashed into the water.

"No! No! No!" I cried. "Joe is going to be so mad and our secret will be out when he asks why I took his eel. Oh! Why did I ever do such a thing! I am going to be in some trouble. I feel sick."

"Oh, I've got an idea, Peggy. Let's see if we can catch it and put it back."

Quickly, getting a line, we baited the hook and lowered it to the bottom beside the wharf where eels would normally hide. Joe's prize eel escaped our line; however, we caught another, much smaller one. Imagine Joe's shock when he went to show off his trophy eel and discovered it was only half the size!

My conscience bothered me so much, I did tell Joe about our fabulous trick but not before making him promise never to say a word to anyone.

Life in the Cove

Life in the cove slowly built inroads into my heart. Simplicity reigned. Time for friends took precedent over getting rich for the majority of residents. Lending a helping hand was considered a privilege, without making the recipient feeling obligated. Some expected pay for everything and a few were nasty. They stuck out like sore thumbs. John and Mary taught us to love and help them just like anyone else.

"Matter of fact," they said, "those people need more love because something is making them unhappy inside."

I know they are wise but it's sure hard to love crabby people, I thought to myself.

Sadie was one of the crabby types. She must have thought she was the protector of the Cove. She tried stopping us from going back to The Swaugh. The Swaugh is the back cove, which is well protected and has lots of sand and warm water. She claimed the path was on her land and not to be crossed. We couldn't figure out what her problem was. Nobody else minded and the right of way had been used for years.

A warm sunny day with high tide was ideal for swimming. Ruby, Sally and I noticed a group of kids heading to The Swaugh for a swim.

"Why don't we go swimming too," I suggested.

Ruby and Sally agreed.

"We'll get changed and meet here in fifteen minutes," Sally said.

Excited about the swim and not seeing Sadie chase the others, we thought she must be busy or sleeping. We were just passing her house when out she came.

"What do you think you're doing on my land? Get off and stay off," she yelled while coming after us waving her broom wildly.

"Let's get out of here, run, run," I yelled. "She might catch us."

We flew like the wind to flee her wrath.

"You won't get away if you come back this way, I promise you," threatened Sadie.

Sally calmed us a bit by saying, "We don't have to run this fast. She is too old to catch us."

"You might be right, but I don't intend to find out," commented Ruby. "She just might hit one of us with that broom and I don't want to be the one."

"How are we going to get past on our way back? Are we going to take the long way around?" I asked.

"No way. We will come with the others and all make a dash past her place before she can catch us," answered Sally. "Now let's enjoy our swim. We can't let Sadie spoil our day."

We did get past her door safely as she didn't attempt to scare us. Maybe it was because a few big boys were with us. We ran past, just as we had planned.

"I was thinking," said Sally. "Have you ever thought about Sadie? She has yet to hit anyone with that broom! Maybe she isn't as crabby as we think. Chasing us may be her way of having fun. We must look pretty funny, running fast as we can while she hobbles behind us waving her broom."

"You may be right," I agreed. "But I'm not waiting to find out."

As it turned out, over the years, more than once she chased us with broom flying and shaking but nobody ever got hit.

With the warmer weather, John, along with the other fishermen, prepared nets and gear for the arrival of mackerel, haddock, and cod. All winter they knitted new nets or made necessary repairs to the old ones. A strong smell in the air told us they were barking nets. I liked that smell. Bark was used to preserve and strengthen rope and twine. Since spruce bark was abundant in the bay, almost every fisherman used it but hickory was sometimes substituted.

Running to John and James, I asked, "Can I help?"

"Yes," John said, "Keep the fire going until the water boils, but be very careful and no running or playing with fire. Do you understand?"

"Oh yes, I'll be very careful," I assured John.

Within half an hour, we had the water boiling and John added bark and tar. The brew, as he called it, was well mixed in the water.

"Okay Peggy, don't put any more wood on the fire. Just let it go out," said James. "Stand back while we put the nets in. We don't want you to get burned."

They carefully lowered the nets into the pot where they would remain until cool enough to handle, over night most likely. The next morning, John and James spread the nets on flat rocks and racks to dry.

"With all this fine weather the nets should dry quickly and be ready to use earlier than usual," said John.

Preparation for the season created much activity at the Cove. Excitement grew each day as the time for fish to arrive got closer. Anchors and brightly painted buoys lined the wharves creating a cheerful atmosphere. Of course, much anticipation in hopes of a great catch permeated the air. Boats were repaired and painted.

When fishing season begins, fishermen rise early. Most set their alarm for four in the morning, giving them time to be at the nets by daybreak. 'Looking the nets' excites every fisherman, especially if the catch is big.

John told us, "You can judge a good catch by the corks. If they're submerged, chances are the net is full. The weight of fish causes the net to sink. Sometimes a shark or two might be caught, submerging the corks and fooling you."

Oft' times, fishermen use trawls which are long lines with smaller lines attached and are about three feet long and three feet apart with baited hooks on the end. Trawls are best for catching ground fish. I remember the first time I heard the term ground fish. I was totally confused.

How could fish live in the ground, I thought?

I didn't want to sound stupid, but curiosity overcame my pride. Finally I asked, "What in the world are ground fish?"

Joe gave me the lowdown. "Ground fish are fish that swim close to the ocean bottom," he explained. "It's just a term to describe the location in which fish like to swim."

Ah! That made sense!

Then there was jigging and hand lining. Jigging had the advantage of not requiring bait. If you went jigging most likely you wanted to catch cod or haddock. Hand lines required bait.

When they had a good catch or finished 'looking the nets', they set sail for home. That's when the fun began for these hearty sea lovers. Racing was the game.

Who could get home first? Southwest winds made it easy as it carried the vessels right into the bay. Getting through the entrance of the cove was the challenge. Sometimes the wind blew straight out the cove, making it necessary to tack before clearing the narrows. More than once, boats struck bottom. A fisherman was considered a great navigator if he got through without ever hitting anything. When safely tied up, the fish were unloaded, cleaned and salted in big barrels called puncheons.

Just before school was over, fishing was at its peak. As I listened to the men telling stories about the good year, I asked John if I could go with them the next day. Miss Smith was going to be away that day, and school had been canceled.

"Yes Peggy, you may come."

I was so excited, that night I went to bed early to get a good sleep.

"Be sure and wake me up, won't you."

"Now don't you worry Peggy, just get a good nights rest, I'll make sure John wakes you early," Mary assured me.

I knew I could rely on her.

John woke me at five. He and James were up earlier and had finished a few chores. We ate a hardy breakfast and set off for the wharf. Some men were sailing out of the Cove while others were arriving. It was a bit chilly with light winds and fog. As we rounded the entrance, swells gently raised and lowered the boat as we cut through the water. This was my first trip on the ocean since the wreck. I tried not thinking about it by keeping my mind on the sun casting beams of light through the lifting fog. Instead of solid fog, it was in patches. We traveled at a steady speed and John guessed we would reach Horseshoe Shoal in about an hour and a half unless the wind changed.

I looked up at the almost totally blue sky and to my surprise, Hector came swooping and squawking over our heads. We laughed at him. James threw a few pieces of bait which caused mad diving as a number of gulls tried to get the prize. Hector won since he was the closest. Two gulls chased him but he did a few fancy maneuvers to lose them and returned to follow us.

Sure enough, we reached the Horseshoe on time as John predicted. I was excited as we neared the first net. It was hardly visible which was a good sign. James gaffed the buoy as we drifted to it.

Looking the Net

"I can see the fish," he shouted with joy, "it's loaded!"

I had to stay back until the sail was taken down and out of the way. They began pulling the net alongside causing the boat to lean as fish flapped everywhere. This was my first experience at 'looking a net'. No wonder they liked it. Carefully removing the fish, it didn't take long to fill loads of boxes. James and John were excited about the great catch. I had never seen men act like this before. The second net was even more loaded than the first. They were practically hysterical. Lastly, was the trawl. A flag on a float high above the water marked it. There are no corks on trawls so you never know whether you have a good catch or not. They started hauling it into to the boat.

John said, "'We've got something big here, I hope it isn't a shark."

"Wow, would you look at the size of that," exclaimed James, as a giant halibut surfaced. "What a beauty!"

John beamed as they slowly brought it to the side and he gaffed it carefully so as not to lose such a treasure. Boy, was it big!

"That must be close to four feet long," John said in awe. "No wonder we were having a hard time pulling the line."

James grabbed the other gaff and both pulled with all their might. Up and over and into the boat it came.

"Boy! We'll have some of that tonight," remarked John with a gleam in his eye. "That's a prize if I do say so."

James agreed.

Winds became stronger as the day wore on, which is normal, but it was warm and sunny. A few other boats were heading back and they reached us by the time we set sail. The three stayed close to each other and the men talked back and forth, asking how their catches were. Every boat was low in the water, indicating a good day of fishing. John was so proud of his halibut he couldn't keep quiet. He and James even held it up for others to see.

"Lucky you," the others said. Then teased him by saying, "Remember we're your good friends."

Harry, in the boat beside us, had his youngest son, Bobby with him. Bobby was tying two small pollock together on a piece of twine about three feet long.

"Watch this Peggy," he called out, as he threw the line with two fish, one on each end.

Flocks of gulls following overhead made a mad dive for the fish as they sailed through the air. There must have been a dozen of them pushing and flapping when the fish hit the water. It was impossible to know which two got them, but not for long. After gulping them down, all but two flew back to the boats looking for another free handout. That's when I realized the truth. One gull tried taking off and that motion jerked the other one half out of the water causing the first one to somersault back into the ocean. They did this a few times. Bobby laughed but I felt sorry for the poor things.

"James," I said, "those birds will be stuck together forever. What shall we do? We can't leave them like that."

"Don't worry Peggy, watch and see."

After a few more attempts to fly away, each gull regurgitated the fish and took off to join the others. As they flew past, they gave dreadful squawks as if scolding Bobby. He laughed harder than ever. I was relieved but didn't think it was as funny as he did.

James said, "That trick is old as the hills, Peggy. I don't know of any boys who haven't tried it."

"Well, I won't and I don't want anyone to ever do that to Hector or I'll, I'll..."

"You'll what, Peggy?"

"I'll get you to beat them up. That's what I'll do. You would do it for me, wouldn't you, James?"

"Well, I don't know if that is a good idea. I wouldn't worry about it unless it happens."

I forcefully replied, "You just remember, I'll be counting on you if they do."

"Maybe I better warn the boys in the Cove, eh?" John joked.

I caught them winking at each other with a little smile, but I meant it!

After all that excitement, we were all quiet for awhile and that's when I remembered the racing home stories.

I hadn't noticed any competition about getting home first like I had expected. Maybe it was because they were so involved with the gull episode. I was just about to ask if we were going to race home when I heard John whisper, "James, adjust the jib while I trim the mainsail."

As we started pulling ahead, I heard the others conspiring in low voices. The challenge was subtle at first but it didn't take long to realize the secret was out. Each skipper at the helm was taking advantage of the waves, riding them to pick up speed. They kept an eye

Entrance to the Cove

on gusts, which darkened the water, trying to catch the wind. I never realized sailing was so complicated. Everyone got into the action saying they were going to beat the pants off the other.

John boasted, "Last one home is a rotten egg."

I had never seen adults act like they were kids. They even wanted John to bet his halibut against them, they were so sure of winning.

"No way", he said, "I'm not a gambler."

Besides, we were gaining even though it was a close race.

As we neared the Cove, it was obvious we were going to be the winners. I was proud of John and James. Coming near the entrance required a tricky maneuver as I mentioned earlier. We almost made it through when a sudden gust came straight at us driving the boat to the right. Try as he might, John couldn't get away from the shore and a gentle bump told we hit the bottom. I felt sick. So did John and James, for John was one of the best navigators who ever sailed through the entrance. The other two boats circled, waiting for us to push off. The unfortunate thing was, we had to turn back to sea to gain enough speed to get through. That gave Harry and Ross the advantage they needed to win. As they sailed past, they smiled and said, "John, what's it like being a rotten egg?"

Then they had the nerve to tell him it was because he had a woman on board. "John, you know its bad luck to take a female fishing."

That's when I really felt bad.

John said, "Peggy, don't be upset. I don't believe in that superstition and besides, it's all in fun. Somebody has to lose. Just look at the good day we had, and, do they have a prize halibut? Would you call that bad luck? I would say you brought us good luck!"

I had to agree but still, I didn't like it. James reminded me about the game of Chinese checkers I won and the lesson John taught me.

"Just look how happy Harry and Ross are after winning," he beamed.

"Okay, I'll try but, I know it's going to be hard, you really had them beat."

There was more razing from the crowd who had seen what happened. As we tied up, however, the attention soon changed direction when the men saw the halibut in the bottom of the boat.

"Wow! Take a look at the size of that," everyone said.

The challenge then went back to Ross and Harry. "Let's see if you can match that, guys."

Everyone laughed while pushing and shoving each other.

John looked my way and nodded with a little smile as if to say, "See, we might have lost the race but we won with the halibut."

I smiled in agreement. At times, communicating without words is best.

After the joking and jesting, everyone got back to the business of cleaning and salting the catch. That's when the gulls filled their bellies. Hector was standing on the side of the splitting table. He'd wait for James or John to hand him the guts, impatient to gobble it down. Gulls were everywhere.

It was way past noon by the time the men went for dinner. With the sun so hot, it was important to get the fish salted before they got soft.

Another nice thing about the community was the willingness to help. Those who finished cleaning and salting their fish helped those who hadn't. I liked to see them working together. It was meant to be that way.

As an example, John did share the halibut with those who helped, even Harry and Ross. I began to see qualities in John that touched my heart. No wonder Mary went out of her way to do extra things for him even when she was extremely busy.

After dinner, John and James had a little rest before working in the garden. Most vegetables were already planted but others couldn't be until after the new moon in June. Frost could destroy certain vegetables.

That was a typical summer day for a fisherman. Other times weren't so fortunate as today. The weather conditions could change suddenly, making it dangerous and sometimes disastrous. On occasion, I wondered how men could face the cold. In order to provide for their families, they had to face extreme elements. At least most men from the Cove were inshore fishermen, and were within a few hours of home. I dreaded the thought of men going to sea for long periods of time and not being with their family every night. Families worried when storms struck before the boats returned.

Toilers of the sea face dangers continually from fog, wind, tide and waves. But not only fishermen have met with tragedy or life threatening experiences at the Cove. Fascinated with powerful waves generated by gale force winds or hurricanes, folks visit here to watch the awesome displays of flying spray and thunderous crashes as waves challenge the cliffs of Peggy's Cove. Too often these innocent spectators have been washed overboard; some never to return, others have been more fortunate.

I remember one particular day just after the eye of a storm passed; many people came to watch the waves. To me it just brought back memories of that terrible night when all were lost, save me. Three teenage boys were letting the wind and spray beat against them with backs to the rocks and faces to the sea. About twenty minutes later, frightened faces showed something was about to happen. One look seaward told the story. Rising beyond anything imaginable was this monster of a wave. Not having time to flee to safety, they ran behind a large rock grabbing a sharp edge for security. They were sure the wave would reach them and held on for dear life. Fortunately for them, the wash didn't come up that far, but others were in a fearful situation. After the wave rushed between them and higher land, voices were heard shouting, "woman overboard". The three boys ran to the crevasse hoping to rescue her. Sure enough, there she was, situated in the crack with a baby in her arms. One boy took her baby and handed it to others who gathered to help. Then two of the boys held her arms and pulled her out. She was hysterical and started calling for her baby.

"We have your baby safe up here," they assured her.

Then, everyone cleared out in a hurry. Her legs were cut, clothes ripped but she was not seriously injured. Thankful that her life was spared, her family escorted her to safety.

As more spectators arrived, gazing at the spectacular seas, locals warned them not to go near the rocks. If only people would listen, but most didn't. A family of four ventured onto the rocks thinking they were safe. Soon another giant wave charged forward, catching them off guard. Some ran to help and managed to rescue the mother and daughter but horror struck instantly as father and son were swept away. Two weeks later their bodies were found. How sad and tragic this loss of life! Again, images raced wildly through my mind as I relived that horrific night in similar weather. Why were they lost and I saved? That question continually rolled through my mind. Would I ever discover my roots and who I was?

Having nothing exciting to do one day, Sally said, "Let's go over to The Dancing Rock. Maybe some kids will be there but if not, we can play hop scotch or sit and watch the waves."

The Dancing Rock

"That's a good idea, the waves are nice today. We need to get a few flat rocks for throwing though, we won't find any there," I replied.

We were allowed to play on The Dancing Rock because it was high from shore. When we arrived, two ladies were seated facing the ocean. They weren't talking, but just sitting enjoying the peacefulness. As we got closer, the ladies turned and spoke to us.

One lady asked, "And who might you two girls be?"

"My name is Sally and this is my best friend Peggy."

"And I am Pat and this is my best friend Alvina."

"You wouldn't happen to be 'Peggy of the Cove' would you?" asked Alvina.

"Yes, that's what a lot of people call me. How did you know?"

"Oh, you have become famous for miles around. I am pleased to meet you after hearing about your survival. You and I have something in common. I too had a near death experience last March."

"Oh wow," said Sally, "Tell us what happened?"

As Alivina began telling her story, cold shivers ran down my back.

"Pat and I came to watch the big waves one day. We thought we were a safe distance to enjoy the surf. I stood close to the edge and turned to look toward Pat. Suddenly, something hit me, knocking me down. What in the world was that? I thought, has someone pushed me? Flying spray and rushing water told the truth. A wave knocked me over. I furiously tried finding a hold in the cracks of the rocks but that didn't work. Backwash pulled me into the ocean, way over my head. Okay, I thought, now I need to get to the bottom to push myself up. But the water was too deep. Then I tried surfacing but that wasn't working either. I felt like a piece of seaweed, swirling whichever way the sea drove me. This isn't working either, I thought, and time is passing. Then another great big wave came, and dragged me farther out to sea. I was disoriented from being rolled and tossed underwater; thinking, Oh my! What is mother going to do? I was convinced drowning was my fate. By now I had given up the fight. Right after thinking that, another wave slammed me against a big rock. At that moment, my head was above water and voices were yelling, "Over here, over here." There is no doubt in my mind that my guardian angel was taking charge of my plight. I turned and saw four boys waving and calling. It was a miracle that I managed to swim over to them while they reached down, grabbed my arms and dragged me to safety. I couldn't believe I never felt the cold water and trust me, on March 19 any year, water at Peggy's is freezing cold. Maybe the coldest of the year! I hadn't swallowed any water and wasn't knocked out which was a miracle considering the forceful wave that smashed my head against solid rock.

"I thanked the four young men profusely. Even though they all introduced themselves, I can't remember their names. After a short conversation, they left.

"The next day I went to work at the hospital because nurses like me never miss a day unless it's impossible to be there. A young intern was shocked when he saw me and asked what happened. The left side of my face, arm, body and leg were black and blue from hitting the rock. Miraculously, only my left eyetooth was broken.

"Since my near-death experience, Peggy's Cove draws me like a strong magnet. I visit for a closer walk with God or whenever I need peace, quietness and energizing. At the time I was only twenty-one years old, and just shook it off, thinking 'Wow! That was a close one.' But, as I get older and especially around the time of the anniversary of that day, I relive my experience no matter how hard I try to obliterate it. Even if I succeed, that week I feel tired and also don't sleep well. My desire is to meet those young boys again and thank them. I'm convinced if they hadn't been there; another wave would have taken me.

"I often go for solitude to this special landmark. It fills a gap in my life."

While telling her story, it's obvious she relives the

experience as she goes through the motions with body and language. There were times when she had to stop; the emotion was too great. Oh, how I relate! We have a special bonding because of our similar experience.

Stewart Manuel wasn't so fortunate. He was in his seventies. Still a toiler of the sea, his net was set off the coast not a long distance from shore. The highlight of his day was 'looking the net'. One fine morning, Stewart rowed out all by himself. He never came back and nobody found him, just an empty boat. There was a shark caught in his net, so most likely he tried bringing it in and either lost his balance or was pulled overboard. Not being able to swim, he probably couldn't get to the boat for safety. That was another sad day.

His wife, Alice, was heartbroken and lived, many years after, to almost one hundred years of age. She loved company and would reminisce for hours entertaining her guests. Greatly loved by the community, she was sadly missed after her death. To most folks, she was known as Aunt Alice.

The Little Yellow Shop

Located at the head of the Cove, on the other side of the road, was a building called the Little Yellow Shop. 'Men Only' wasn't posted on the door but it might just as well have been. Women were forbidden to enter. Rarely would any female even knock on the door. 'Emergencies' or 'important matters only' was the unwritten rule that would allow the presence of a lady. The person requested would come out rather than invite a woman in.

One warm evening, having nothing to do, Sally and I let our minds run to a mischievous mood.

"Did you ever wonder what men talk about in the Little Yellow Shop?" I questioned.

"I surely do."

"You would think the place was sacred the way men folk went on. All they ever do is sit around spinning yarns, smoking or chewing tobacco or playing a game of cards or checkers. I can't figure out what is so special about the place. Can you, Sally?"

"No, I don't know either, would you like to find out?"

"Yes, of course," I replied with a grin.

"Let's sneak around back and listen through the window."

I was a little nervous for fear of getting caught but agreed anyway. We glanced around, making sure the coast was clear before quietly hiding between the building and some large puncheons a few feet away. They provided a great shield from the neighbours. Dusk helped make us almost invisible.

The Little Yellow Shop

Just as we arrived, laughter bellowed through the open window. We didn't hear the tale, but it must have been a good one because they were splitting their sides for a long time.

Shortly after everyone settled down, Clyde, who had just arrived from West Dover, was anxious to tell his story. "Did you fellows hear about Tom and the rum?" he asked.

"No, but it sounds like a good one if Tom was involved. What happened? Tell us, Clyde."

Sally and I thought this would be worth hearing as he began the story.

"Tom helped one of the bootlegger families unload a shipment of rum. He and the family involved were the only ones who knew where it was hidden. Tom was staying with his father down in Pollock Cove for the summer. The other night when Tom was sure his father was asleep, he got up and walked from Pollock Cove to Seabright, through the old Dover Road."

Pollock Cove

"Really," Roger mused, "that must be eight miles or more."

"Yeah, you're right about that," they all agreed.

"He took a keg of rum and hid it in a different spot. Then returned home, sneaked back into the house and to bed before his father was even awake.

"Upon the discovery of the missing keg of rum, the Duffy family was out to get Tom, since he was the only other person who knew where their rum was hidden.

Down they went to give Tom a little visit. Of course, Tom denied it and his father backed up his story. He swore an oath, "It wasn't Tom, he was here when I went to bed and here when I got up". The Duffy's weren't happy but believed Tom's father since he was known for his honesty. If not for his father, Tom would have paid for his theft dearly."

"We better keep this one to ourselves, boys," Clyde said, "or the Duffy's will pound the tar out of Tom." They all agreed.

Although Tom didn't get a beating, or worse, because of his father's defense, he was guilty. I didn't think it was worth the consequences. Would Sally and I be in trouble if anyone discovered we listened? I began to wish we had kept our noses clean.

My mind recalled the fine principles John and Mary instilled in me; one was to stay away from alcohol. The common name was rum or booze. Some had their own stills hidden in the woods or on an island. Hearing of family quarrels, breakups and abuse from the use of alcohol, I was determined to have nothing whatsoever to do with anyone involved in that line of business. Not only that, it was against the law.

Rum running was common along the coast. Large schooners were used to bring kegs of rum close to shore in secluded coves or islands, they were rolled up the beach and then well hidden among thick brush or trees.

The tales continued as we listened outside. Ralph said he had a good one to tell. "You fellows know Billy Harnish, right?"

"Yeah, why?"

"Well, two of his grandchildren paid a nasty trick on him. Ada found Bill's rum hidden in the grass under a tree. She told Walter and between the two of them they thought of a plan. They knew how snakes terrified him.

I'm not sure if you fellows know it or not, but big snakes are always in the field near Bill's house. They searched for a big one but couldn't find any, so had to settle for a small feller. They tied it to his bottle of rum with a piece of thread and waited until it was time for him to come home from work. Then they placed the bottle of rum on the path so he would be sure to see it and waited to see what he would do. Sure enough, he saw the rum and bent down to pick it up. Well! He threw it down as fast as he could when the snake came up at him. Again he reached for the rum, thinking he would grab it before the snake could get near him. Snatching up the bottle he was scared half-to-death as the snake flew towards him again. Away went the rum the second time. After a number of tries, Bill finally figured out what was going on but not before Walter and Ada had a good laugh."

The tales continued no doubt, but Sally and I were overdue at our homes. Perhaps, we told each other, we'll come again and hear more from the Little Yellow Shop. Although I chuckled at the time, on the way home, I kept thinking about how alcohol makes people act so foolish. If that would have been John, would I have thought it funny?

Uncle Willie's Blacksmith Shop

At dinnertime, John explained, "I'm going to Willie Boutilier's blacksmith shop tomorrow to pick up some anchors. Along the way I'll deliver fish and grit to a few families." With a twinkle in his eye, he said, "Would you like to go along?"

"Yes," I answered, "you know how I love new places. Is anyone else coming with us?"

"Not yet. Maybe someone will change their mind."

I was hoping Joe would come along but he had made plans with two other boys to build a raft and play pirates. He promised to help them or he would have come with us.

I jumped at the opportunity and was so excited I could hardly sleep that night just thinking about it. Stories about this blacksmith and his fascinating shop excited me. Now the opportunity to see his shop for myself wouldn't be just a wish. Uncle Willie had many nieces and nephews I would meet. Not only was he Uncle Willie to his relatives but to every young person. Grownups simple called him Willie. He lived on MacDonald's Point in Seabright, about ten miles up the road. People said he was a gentle, kind man, but his clothes were as black as coal from the soot and smoke. His long white beard looked like someone took a pepper shaker to it. Kids loved working the bellows creating fiery coals that turned the metal red-hot.

You may have noticed I mentioned John was going to deliver grit. For those not familiar with grit, it is ground up shells fed to chickens. They have gizzards instead of stomachs and grit breaks down the food so they can digest it. The ocean makes grit. As shellfish wash ashore, waves crush them against the rocks breaking them into small pieces. The best grit is found on Ironbound Island, a few miles off Peggy's Cove, because open sea pounds the shore and there are tons of shells.

Morning finally arrived and after a big breakfast the horse and wagon were hitched up, supplies loaded and off we went. The weather was simply beautiful. Hector and his seagull friends swooped over us looking for a free meal, crows cawed, warning all creatures we were coming. Other birds sang their hearts out as if competing to see who could sing the loudest, most beautiful song. Passing through Indian Harbour, the next village, folks waved and commented about the great day. Fishermen were cleaning and salting their catch.

Monday was wash day throughout the Bay so ladies were hanging out their laundry. The big competition was to have the nicest looking clothesline. Size, colour, and order in which clothes were hung, showed the neighbours you knew what you were doing. If a woman didn't do it right, they would be the talk of the town that day. Also, it was a big thing to get your wash out first. The talk was some women got up before daybreak like the men. It was a known fact that a few would cheat by doing part of their wash the night before so they could have it out first. Using a scrub board was slow work and with large families, washday was a major job. If you saw all those clotheslines you would have to admit it was a pretty sight. How grand life was in this peaceful setting!

After going through a stretch called The Harbour Woods, we came to the top of Jim Ernst's hill.

"What a gorgeous view, I never tire of seeing it, don't you agree, John?"

"Yes Peggy, it's like being on top of the world."

"That's funny, I was thinking the same thing. Just look at Hackett's Cove below with Luke's, Troop's, and Moser's Islands nestled on the east side of the bay. Isn't that breathtaking?"

He agreed, "You are absolutely right Peggy."

A few more turns in the road and we would be at our first stop, Sherman Covey's.

Wow! What a climb it was to reach their house. This was the longest, highest hill that I could ever remember climbing.

"We best let the horse rest a few times before reaching the top," John suggested.

"Can you imagine going up and down this hill at least four times every day for school alone?"

"No, not really, but it would keep you in shape."

Fortunately for the Covey kids, the school was just below the hill on the opposite side of the road. Everybody went home for dinner so that's why the four trips a day. What exercise that was climbing a mountain so often.

"Boys oh boys, look at that view John, isn't that something."

"That's right, you can see clearly from Shut-in-Island to Tantallon as well as the entire west coast of St. Margaret's Bay."

There were more islands than I thought.

Sport, the family dog, met us first and was so friendly you could almost see a smile on his face. He looked like a collie but was black and white. Then two girls appeared which had its good and bad points.

Getting to know people was becoming easier and always having so much fun it was worth the effort. A tall, stately man came down from the barn. That must be Sherman, better known as Grandpop. Then Lalia was introduced as Grammy. That's what the local kids called her. They had four girls and four boys.

Victoria and Evelyn, who I met first, asked me to come over to Simon's Rock and play with them. Effie was there already. Frances, I learned was not home.

On our way, I asked, "Why is it called Simon's Rock?"

"They laughed and said, "Simon used to get into the spirits. When he drank too much alcohol, his wife wouldn't let him in the house so he would go and sleep under the shelter of this big rock. So it became known as Simon's Rock."

"Wow, it is big," I agreed.

I met Effie and we talked for a few minutes.

Just then four boys came out of the woods returning from Corney's Lake and had a mess of trout.

"Come Peggy, meet our brothers." Victoria said.

They were showing John their great catch.

Victoria said, "Boys, this is Peggy. Peggy, this is Willie, Jimmy, Harold and Raymond."

"We're glad to meet you, Peggy. We heard lots about you. How do you like living in Peggy's Cove? What do you think of the view? Where are you headed?"

Wow, too many questions, I thought. It was hard to keep the right name with the right face. They all knew who I was. Seems they were fascinated to meet this well-known, "Peggy of the Cove", who miraculously survived the shipwreck. I thought it funny, them paying attention to little old me. We bade our good-byes and left.

Going down the hill would be too steep for the horse with a loaded wagon, so John chained one of the wheels to the frame. That acted like a brake or I'm sure we would have had the cart before the horse by the time we reached the bottom.

"They're nice people, aren't they?" I said to John.

"Yes, they're a fine family."

"Tell me, what does Grandpop do?"

"Well, he's a fisherman like a lot of other men folk. He grows a fine crop of vegetables, as his land is some of the most fertile along the bay. His father was a wheelwright and taught Sherman the trade as well. Did you notice the dip nets the boys had from their fishing trip?"

"Well, I saw them but didn't pay attention to them."

"Grandpop made them and if you had looked closely you would have found perfection. He also makes and mends sails. Every piece of work he produces is done with the touch of a craftsman.

"Some time ago an illness prevented him from working at his trade. For two years, minor jobs requiring very little effort were all he could do. Those were difficult times for these folks. There wasn't enough money to support his family. The boys did what they could to provide food but some things just had to be bought. The storeowner, Everet Shatford of Indian Harbour, gave him the necessary items on charge. If it hadn't been for Everet's kindness and trust, I don't know how they would have survived. Grandpop was very grateful and started repaying the debt after getting well. It took him ten years before all was paid off."

Back on the road again, it wasn't long before we met someone coming toward us.

"See that fellow coming down the road, that's William Covey."

"Yes, he's a small man. What about him?"

"Do you want to hear a story about William?"

"Of course I do, I love stories."

"William came to this area from LaHave, which is near Mahone Bay, and was looking to buy property. A man named Bowie had a house for sale. William said he would buy it if he had the money. Sherman's great grandfather, James Covey, offered to lend him the money. On his way to buy the house, William wanted to look his best but didn't have a suit. James offered his suit as well. There was only one problem. James was a big man and William, as you can see, is small. Well, he put the suit on anyway. James had to smile as he told William he looked like a parson's shirt on a handspike."

In case you don't know what a handspike is, it's a crowbar like tool, used by fishermen.

Traveling up the road, we came to Glen Margaret and then Seabright. In Glen Margaret, I was excited to pass the Fraser home.

John said, "On the way back home we are going to have supper with them."

I know you will be pleased about that since you're good friends with Janet."

"Oh that's great, how come you didn't tell me?"

"I thought it might be nice to surprise you. I just couldn't keep it a secret any longer. I wasn't going to tell you until we drove in."

"Well I'm glad you did, now I can look forward to having fun with Janet."

Everybody along the way seemed so friendly and relaxed. John knew everyone; at least that's the way it looked to me.

I asked repeatedly, "When will we get there?"

He gave me the same answer every time, "Soon."

"Soon", I said, "You've been telling me that since the first time I asked."

"Yes, you and every young person always want to know when we are going to get there, wherever we are going. Be patient and enjoy the scenery."

Okay I'd try but soon was a long time to me. Finally we turned left at MacDonald's Point. Now I was getting anxious.

"How do you like the winding road?"

"It's a pretty place, especially at the bottom of this steep hill. Isn't that a cute little cove with sand coming up close to the road."

"You're right Peggy, it's hard to find a prettier spot than St. Margaret's Bay. Look how clear the water is. The warm water is so inviting it has enticed the neighbourhood kids to swim and play with boats I would say."

A few came running toward us asking, "Can we get a ride to Uncle Willie's?"

"Sure, jump on," said John. "What's your name?" "Mine is John and this is Peggy."

"Mine is Melvin and this is David."

"And who is the little fellow that can hardly walk?" John asked.

"His name is Willard, he's our little brother."

"You need to be a little more careful. I saw you each had one of his arms but his feet were dragging more than walking as you caught up to the wagon. You wouldn't want to hurt him." John stopped as they hopped on.

It didn't take long to reach the blacksmith shop from the little cove.

As we rounded the last bend, I couldn't help but say, "Wow! Look at all that black smoke billowing from the chimney, is the place on fire?"

"Oh no," piped up David, "That's the way Uncle Willy works. There's always lots of smoke when he's

Uncle Willie's Blacksmith Shop

making stuff. You'll soon see what's going on inside."

I don't know where they came from but all of a sudden there were kids everywhere. David and Melvin introduced me to them but I couldn't remember all those names.

They grabbed my hand and said, "Come on, let's watch Uncle Willie make stuff."

Inside was more shocking than I had imagined.

"How does he breathe in there? Look at all the smoke. It's not only going out the chimney, it's in the shop as well, and so thick I can taste it. Is it safe to go inside?"

Almost instantly the choice was made for me as I was pulled over to the forge and introduced to Uncle Willie. Everything I had heard was true, his black clothes, peppered white beard and kind face. His voice was gentle as he gave me a wonderful smile and a loving handshake. He was a Christian man.

He said, "I am pleased to meet you, Peggy.
Everyone in the Bay has heard about you. "I'm sure God
has something special in mind for your life. Make sure
you spend time with Him every day."

"Thank you, I heard a lot about you too. Tell me, is
it always this smoky?"

He smiled while speaking, in his quiet, calm voice,
"Yes, it's smoky here isn't it. Whenever I work the forge,
it gets pretty black. I'm used to it but most folks find it
rather hard to breathe.

"Time seems to stand still here," he said as he
stopped his work to show me how the bellows make the
coals red hot. You can watch me while I hammer the iron
on the anvil."

The tools were simple but he did marvelous work
with them. It was a fascinating place.

Just then we noticed a boat landing on the beach. A
young man came up to the shop.

Uncle Willie said, "Floyd, I'd like you to meet Peggy."

"Well Peggy, how nice to meet you. Have you met a
lot of new friends?"

"Yes, so many I can't remember all their names, but
I'm learning."

"Floyd is from Fox Point, almost directly across the
Bay from you Peggy," explained Uncle Willie. "Now if
you will excuse me, I'll get Floyd's hoe and saws."

Uncle Willie found a hoe he had made for Floyd
and a few saws that he sharpened.

Floyd said, "Uncle Willie this is the finest hoe I've
ever seen. How much do I owe you?"

I didn't hear the amount but Floyd replied, "That's
not enough for a fine piece of work like that."

Then a strange thing happened. Uncle Willie started
to get upset as he said, "Floyd, that is the price and I
don't want a penny more."

"If you insist," Floyd agreed, "But it is worth a lot more."

So to keep him happy, Floyd paid the small price. Talk had it that Uncle Willie was noted for not charging enough for the work he did. That was just his way of doing business.

I learned relatives sometimes brought bread or sweets to Uncle Willie and cleaned his living quarters. He would not think of taking money from their husbands when he did a job for them. He'd just quietly say, "That work has already been paid for."

Melvin and David grabbed my hands while saying, "Come outside."

"Thank you for getting me out of the smoke, it was starting to bother me."

"That's okay, do you want to hear a few stories about Uncle Willie. We didn't want to say anything in front of him."

"Sure, I would love to. What do you know, Melvin?"

"One day, Uncle Willie was helping the men take a large catch of tuna out of the trap. The spiller, which is a large, strong net made of rope, is used to prevent the trap from being destroyed when the tuna try to escape. Somehow, as they were placing it, the boat leaned quite far and Uncle Willie fell overboard. There he was bobbing around in the trap with all those tuna. He couldn't swim very well either, and was having an extra hard time with heavy clothing and big rubber boots. The men managed to grab his arms and pull him to safety. That was a little to close for comfort for Uncle Willie."

"Boy, he could have been really hurt, what a scary thing. Is there anything Uncle Willie can't do?"

David said, "Oh I'm sure there must be something but not too much. Floyd often says he is a genius.

"Robie Boutilier was known as Robie Dick, Dick being his father's first name. Folks called a lot of families by their father's first name to distinguish which Boutilier family they were talking about. That was common in the Bay area.

"Anyway, Robie had a piece of equipment that had a broken gear. He tried to get a new one but had no success from the supplier or manufacturer. Finally he went to Uncle Willie, hoping he could do something. Well, he told Robie to leave it on the bench and he would see what he could do. Sometime later, he got around to finding just the exact piece of metal, drilled and shaped it just right. Then with a file, he worked endlessly until the teeth matched the broken one perfectly. Robie came to pick up the new gear. The price was so low Robie didn't think he charged enough to buy a new file but Uncle Willie wouldn't take a penny more. He said, "that would do just fine." When Robie put the new gear in place, he was amazed that it worked as good as if it was factory made. A lot of people said Uncle Willie was a genius. Robie sure thought he was."

"How does he live if he doesn't charge much money for his work?" I asked.

"I guess it's because all he ever does is work. He is here early in the morning and works late at night.

"One day a man arrived at the blacksmith shop wanting a railing. He was from Halifax. Uncle Willie agreed to make it and worked away at his usual relaxed pace. A rush job was something he never did. Upon completion the fellow came to pick it up and wondered if he had enough money. When he asked the cost, Uncle Willie told him a price and the man insisted it was worth ten times that. He too tried to give more but failed to persuade Uncle Willie.

A gentleman from the United States somehow

found Uncle Willie's blacksmith shop, which fascinated him as much or more than it does we who know him. He couldn't believe the fine work Uncle Willie did with the crude tools. The gentleman coaxed and pleaded for Uncle Willie to move to the United States and work for him in his machine shop."

Uncle Willie said in a slow voice, "This is just fine here for me."

"Peggy, did you ever meet or hear about Borden Longard?"

"I haven't met him but at the Cove, when someone's watch isn't working, folks say, "take it to Borden, he'll fix it."

"Genius must run in the family because Borden and Uncle Willie are first cousins. Borden mostly repairs watches but he too could do almost anything when it came to mechanical devices. He was invited to the United States to work as well, but he, too, said he liked the neighbours here. You should see the little steam engine he made. It actually works. It's so tiny I don't know how he made it," David explained.

"You sure know a lot about everyone, David, I hope I can remember people like that."

After doing all our business at Uncle Willie's we headed for home. About a mile down the road was the Seabright School, which had a pond at the back. John decided to stop and let the horse have a good drink. A few kids were playing a game I had never heard of before.

"Want to join us in a game?" a girl asked.

"I guess so," I said timidly, "if you tell me how."

"Sure, but first, what's your name? I'm Virginia Boutilier."

"I'm Peggy."

"Really," she said, "Are you Peggy of the Cove?"

"Well yes, some have called me that."

"Oh, we are so excited to meet you. Effie and Sue told us you were at Janet Fraser's on the Easter holidays. They told us how much fun you all had telling stories about school days.

"I forgot, this is Kathleen and Sylvia Hubley, they are my best friends," Virginia said.

They were excited to meet me and knew all about my story. Seeing the look on my face told them I really didn't want to talk about it so we got started playing right away.

Virginia explained the rules. "The game was Duck," she said. "See that big rock, that's the Granny Rock. The person who is 'it' has to place their rock on top of the Granny Rock. Then we stand behind that line and throw our rocks at it. The idea is to knock it off the Granny Rock. After knocking it off, we run and collect our rocks and head back to the starting line. The person who is 'it' has to take their rock, place it back on the Granny Rock and try tagging someone before they collect theirs and get back to the starting line. If they tag someone, that person is then 'it'. Do you get it?"

"I think so, but if not, you can tell me as we play."

Virginia said, "The danger is getting your fingers hit in the scurry of the game."

They said it hurt but the game was so much fun it was worth it. She and some of the others showed me their bruised fingers.

Of course, being new at this and a bit slow on the run, after a few throws, I was caught and became 'it'. The horse was finished drinking by now but John just sat in the wagon and watched. I finally caught Sylvia and soon after John motioned for me to come.

"I would love to stay but we have to leave. Thank you for including me."

Kathleen said, "You're welcome Peggy. Whenever you are up this way be sure and stop at our house. You could play with us while John goes on to Uncle Willie's."

"That would be nice. We'll see. Bye for now and thanks again."

"Bye," they all said. Say hello to Janet for us."

"Okay, I will."

It was wonderful to meet more friendly kids. They really made me feel special.

John said, "Now we will head for the Fraser home. We'll have a good supper there."

"My, that sounds good as I was looking forward to a hot meal. Those sandwiches were great, but I'm starved now. Can we hurry?"

Janet was waiting for me outside. She was sitting on a swing. It was tied to a large, overhanging branch of

Janet's House

a big ash tree. We had only a few minutes to play while the men unloaded the wagon. We arrived just in time for supper. The table was large to accommodate the family. Nobody seemed to mind the crowd and all chatted while eating.

"That was a fine meal", John said, "We're staying to bring in the last load of hay. It's going to rain tomorrow and you'll need all the help you can get."

"Well John, you don't really have to do that," said Mr. Fraser, "but yes, it would be a big help. Thank you very much. But first let's take a few minutes to let our stomachs rest."

The men didn't wait too long before they headed to the field.

What fun we had riding the hay wagon up the hill and loading it. We kids laughed while jumping to see who could do the best job of 'tramping' the hay. 'Tramping' was jumping on it or 'tramping it down' so more could be taken in a load. I couldn't believe the amount of hay that was finally loaded on the wagon. It was so high it was scary.

"Come on you kids, I'll help the rest of you get on the wagon," Mr. Fraser said.

Down the hill we headed. Then two things happened at the same time. One little fellow was in a crab apple tree and got his foot caught while scampering down to get a ride to the barn. He was yelling and crying because by now he was upside down with his foot in the crutch of two branches. I believe it was his mother who went to his rescue and brought him safely to his feet again. Meanwhile, Mr. Fraser was at a very steep drop in the hill and was going very slowly to avoid tipping. Too late! Slowly the wagon started rolling over. We screamed while flying through the air and were buried in the hay. My mind flashed to the night of the shipwreck that had tossed and covered me in the sea. It was dark in the hay as well. Adults were digging furiously to get us out. Quickly, they counted to make sure all were there and okay. Fortunately, nobody was hurt. The tongue on the wagon was twisting so badly the poor oxen had their heads turned at an awful angle. Mr. Fraser quickly unyoked them to set them free. They didn't get hurt either.

He said, "That's enough for today. I have some large tarps to cover the hay and I'll get to it tomorrow, hopefully before the rain starts."

We kids and adults agreed since we all were shaken from the experience. The men, with help from the oxen tipped the wagon back on its wheels before leaving.

I was happy to be on our way home again even though I had met so many wonderful people. We passed folks taking evening strolls along the way but John didn't stop. He waved or spoke as we drove by. Neither of us said much on the last leg home. Dusk arrived as we drove in the yard.

John said, "You go inside and get ready for bed. I'll take care of the horse and be in shortly."

Mary came out to meet us and asked, "How was your day, Peggy?"

I talked a mile a minute telling her of my adventures while getting ready for bed. Then as I settled down, I realized I was beat.

Lying in bed was such sweet rest and I relived the highlights of the day. Then my mind was saddened as I thought about my lost parents, who I was and where I came from. If only I could remember beyond the wreck. I prayed every day for answers. Would God hear? A tear slowly rolled down my cheek as I fell into a deep sleep.

James Heads to Sea

With school days behind him, James remained home until haying was finished and a good supply of winter wood was cut, split and piled. The possibility of going to sea with Captain Simms was becoming more of a sure thing as each week passed. It was almost certain he would be leaving soon.

A letter from the Captain arrived and James opened it with excitement. Sure enough, he was hired and would be starting work in about two weeks. Captain Simms was waiting for a new sail and doing repairs so James would have a little time before leaving. The letter informed James that a load of lumber from a mill at the head of the Bay would be dropped off at the Cove. If he would be ready, he could leave from there without travelling to Seabright. Everyone agreed that would be a good idea.

Excited as everyone was, and I did feel happy for him, a void grew in my heart. I had become dependent on James for advice and protection. He was always there whenever I needed a word of encouragement. Maybe we got along so well because I replaced the void left by the loss of Elizabeth.

One thing surprised me early the next morning as I was coming to the top of the stairs. I don't know why, but I stopped to look out the window at the beautiful day and heard James speak to Mary. "Mother," he hesitated.

"Yes James, is something on your mind? I can always tell when you are thinking seriously."

"Yes, as a matter of fact, there is. You know Peggy remembers very little of her past, and I was wondering what we should do about her birthday?"

"Oh yes James, you're right. I, too, thought about it, but never said anything."

"Well, I was thinking it might be a nice thing if we celebrated her birthday on the same day as Elizabeth's. What's your opinion? Or would that cause too much hurt?"

"Why, no, James, that's a splendid idea. I'm sure your father and the boys would love it too. Why don't I ask them just in case they don't feel the same way? I could suggest it to Peggy and find out her thoughts as well. That means we could have a party before you leave."

When Mary asked if I liked the idea I was quite excited about it. "July 17, I don't know why, but there is something familiar about that date. Oh well, it doesn't matter, thank you Mary for being so kind."

"Don't thank me, Peggy, James is the one who spoke to me about your birthday and suggested we use Elizabeth's birth date. We all approved and I was asked to speak to you in private to make sure you were comfortable with it."

"Mary, everyone has been so good to me. Aside from my real Mother and Father, there is no better family I could have chosen even if I would have done so myself."

"Peggy, you're a joy to have as part of our family,

we all have been blessed. I thank God every day for bringing a girl back into our home."

The next few days were filled with excitement as the birthday party grew and grew and grew. At first I thought it was only a family party, but each of the boys wanted to have a few friends and Mary said I could invite whoever I wanted. John insisted the men who helped rescue me be there too. Then the ladies who fed and warmed me wanted to come as well. Finally, Mrs. Crooks spoke up and said, "Why not make this a community celebration? That way everyone can enjoy the party. Let's call it the birthday of 'Peggy of the Cove.'" Everyone agreed, so it was settled.

The plan was to gather on Sunday, shortly after noon. The Dancing Rock was first suggested but if the whole community showed up, there wouldn't be enough space and the older folks wouldn't be able to climb, so Mary invited them to use our yard.

I was overwhelmed by the commotion of a birthday celebration. After all, lots of kids had birthdays in the Cove without a fuss like this. "This is different," they said. "You are a miracle child and have brought joy back into Mary's family and the community loves you as well. We all feel like we are your parents. So we want to celebrate and make this a big event. Besides this gives us an excuse to get together as a community. We need to do it more often."

After a talk like that I didn't have a leg to stand on so I let them do what they wanted. I did ask Mary if she would make sure nobody put me on the spot. I didn't want to be embarrassed in front of everyone in the village.

She said, "Don't worry Peggy, we'll make sure that doesn't happen. After all, this is supposed to be your day and a happy one at that."

Sunday arrived with a clear blue sky after two days of rain. The Cove was a busy place with men carrying tables, chairs, and a large streamer that said, "Happy Birthday, Peggy of the Cove." My friends made flags with happy birthday greetings as well. Lots of people were hurrying because church started at 11:00 o'clock. That meant they had to have everything ready before church so they could be at our place on time afterwards.

Mary called, "Peggy, come here please. I need you for a minute." When I walked through her bedroom door, my eyes almost popped out of my head. Hanging behind the door was a beautiful blue and white dress. "Happy birthday, Peggy, I hope you like it"

"Like it," I squealed, "It's beautiful! Now I know why you have been up so late the last few nights. You were doing this to surprise me. Oh! Mary, I love you!" Both of us had moist eyes as we hugged.

"You are welcome Peggy. It's rewarding to make things for someone who appreciates it so much."

After church, people came from every direction. Food with fancy trimmings was overflowing the tables. There was sauerkraut, turnip kraut, fish chowder, solomon gundy, pickled beets, freshly baked bread, and corn beef and cabbage for starters. The desserts were fabulous and included blueberry pie (made from preserved blueberries), rhubarb pies, apple pies, fresh strawberries and cream and molasses cookies. Mary finally settled everyone and asked the minister to give the Blessing. We could take whatever food we liked. What a feast! This was one happy party. I couldn't believe they did all this for me. Then James disappeared into the house and came out with my cake. Actually, there were many cakes, because one would have been much too small for all the guests. They sang "Happy Birthday" to me and then everyone clapped and cheered.

Mary gave me a knife to cut the cake after making a wish. I thanked them all for being so kind and hoped I could make them as happy as they made me. All the kids played a number of games while the adults cleaned up and sat around chatting. All in all it was a most wonderful day. It was late afternoon before the Cove settled back to normal. I never would forget my first birthday party at the Cove!

The next few days flew as James prepared to leave. Talk around the table was positive as they discussed how he would see new ports throughout the Maritimes. Joe asked if he was going to have a girl in every port. They all laughed.

"No, I don't think so," he replied, "we'll be sleeping on the ship."

"Sure you will," laughed Peter. "Tell us another one."

Mary spoke with a smile but also a serious look; "You treat the women like ladies, if you do meet any, James."

"Aw, come on Mother, you know better than that."

"Well I'm just reminding you. You know how young men get when they are together away from home."

Joe piped up, "That's right Mom, you tell him." Even though all the talk was joking and well meaning, I had a feeling something was going to be missing when James left.

The following Thursday afternoon, a large schooner approached the entrance to the Cove. No doubt this was Captain Simms. Adults and children gathered to see this large schooner and to wish James farewell and a safe voyage.

It took the remainder of the day to unload the lumber and other supplies. Captain Simms told James to have supper at home and come aboard later. The rising tide would make it easier to sail. The next stop was not far away and they could make it to Tancook Island before dark with the long summer evenings. The Tancookers wanted the schooner docked by sunrise at the latest to exchange supplies and cargo. We all hugged James as we bid him good-bye and wished him safe traveling. Suddenly I began feeling weepy so made my farewell quickly with a brave smile. I ran home and sat on my favourite rock down by the shore. Hector arrived saying hello in his gull language. He brought comfort as I watched the schooner pick up speed pointing west toward Tancook Island. "James," I thought, "be careful and come back soon." As I watched James sail away, something deep within my mind awakened a faint memory.

James Goes to Sea

The End